The Home Grown Terrorist

Love, Sex, and Romance in the Backwoods of America

by **John Tomikel**

ISBN 978 0 910042 -73-4

1. The Mountaineer Militia

"What the hell happened?"

It was an angry Earl Hazzard asking Flint, his right hand man, about an event in Charleston, the capital city of West Virginia. Flint went on to describe the situation as best he could.

"You know I gave Fred a ride to Charleston. He seemed real nervous and I could not understand that. I had no idea what he was up to. We were just going to deliver the sheep, pick up some cheap feed and come right back home. He acted strange and said he wanted to go to the political rally and if we didn't connect he would catch the bus back when it was over. I ran into Jimmy Critchlow who was in the capital and we decided to go over and see what Marcia Butler had to say. I figured I would wait for Fred and after the rally give him a ride back. "

Earl looked at Flint. "Well describe the event. All I got was the sketchy television coverage."

Flint took a deep breath and exhaled. "Fred was at the platform where the representative Marcia Butler was going to address the crowd. We split up after we parked and if it wasn't for Jimmy, I wouldn't have been there. Fred went on up to where the platform had been constructed and I went to deliver the sheep and pick up the feed. After I made the delivery and picked up the feed I ran into Jimmy and he talked me into going to the rally. We were back a ways from the speaker platform, but we could see Fred right up front."

"How close was Fred to the microphone?"

"I would say, maybe fifteen feet."

"Close enough for even a woman with poor eyesight to get a good shot."

Flint nodded and thought the comment strange. "Well, this woman came out and stepped up to the microphone and Fred must have thought it was Marcia Butler and shot her in the chest and she dropped immediately. Fred should have known it was someone that was going to introduce Marcia. I guess he wasn't thinking straight and was nervous. Can't blame Fred too much for the mistake, since the woman had the same build as Marcia and the same kind of hairdo. I don't understand why Fred did it. But, I'm sure he was after Marcia."

"Dammit, we looked at videos of Marcia at least fifty times and he should have been able to recognize her. Hell, she's on local television every night spouting off all that environmental nonsense. What happened after that, TV says he shot a couple of other people."

"Yeah, he just kept blasting. He even got off a round in my direction. You seem to know Fred's intent. Did you send him on a mission?"

"No, of course not. But, I knew his intent. He was going to shoot Marcia, surrender and while the cameras were on him, make a statement he should have memorized. Don't tell anyone I told you that."

"My lips are sealed." Flint continued with the story. "After Fred unloaded his pistol, a security policeman moved in. Fred raised his hands in surrender and the policeman shot him right between the eyes. Actually, not between the eyes, but in the forehead. Fred dropped like a sack of oats."

"Did he have any message on him? I guess he didn't get a

4

chance to say anything."

Earl's questions and reaction to the events seemed to be confusing to Flint. "Well it didn't do him any good. If he had a written message then I guess they will find the transcript when they search the body."

Earl Hazzard took another swig of his beer. His eyes seemed to blaze with fury. "Where did the cop get off shooting Fred when, as you say, he raised his hands in surrender."

"Fred didn't drop the gun. His hands were in the air and he still had the pistol in his right hand. I'm sure people will testify to that."

"Goddam trigger happy cops. I guess the cop will get away with shooting Fred, maybe even get a promotion."

It was Flint's opinion that he or Earl would have to talk to Fred's sister Mavis. "She will be blaming our organization, and rightly so."

"We can assure her it was Fred's idea and we didn't have anything to do with it. Fred was just fed up with government interference with his life and was trying to make a statement to that effect."

"Well, I certainly didn't have anything to do with it." assured Flint. " I just drove him to Charleston."

Hazzard looked directly at Flint. "I didn't have anything to do with it either. Just remember that when the cops start asking questions."

Flint shook his head. "Well, Fred might have been able to make his statement if he hadn't turned the pistol on the crowd. It

5

might make sense to shoot a government official and make your claim, but it would not be a valid claim if you shot up innocent people standing by."

"You know your problem Flint."

"What's that Guppy?"

"You try to see both sides of every issue. I don't question that you are a patriot, but I don't like the idea of you're trying to analyze our actions from the other point of view."

"I figure you have to know what the enemy is thinking and I put myself in the position of the enemy in order to insure my own thoughts are not way out."

"Also, don't call me Guppy. That was okay when we were growing up, but now we are adults."

"What should I call you. I've always known you as Guppy, since we were kids."

"Call me Earl, or better yet, address me as Captain."

Okay. I'll call you Captain when we are on duty and Earl when we are just being social, how's that?"

"That would be fine lieutenant."

Flint had one last comment. "Fred shouldn't have initiated such violence, we could get our message across without the violence."

"It takes violence to get someone's attention. You can picket for years and nobody will give you a second look. You're right, I should discuss clandestine actions with some of the more trustworthy members. Extra input is always welcome." From that Flint gathered that he might not be considered as a trustworthy member.

Earl Hazzard was the leader of The Mountaineer Militia, a small militia band located in the hills of central West Virginia. Interstate 50 ran right through the middle of their bailiwick which encompassed hills and valleys of three different counties. Earl was thirty six years old and George "Flint" Holaway was thirty four. Earl was married and had two children. Flint was married to Marjorie who took off one night without saying a word. Flint received a postcard from Florida with the message , "Glad you're not here." Flint never received any divorce papers so he assumed he was still married to Marjorie despite the five year absence. There was no need to get a divorce, he wasn't going anywhere.

Flint got his nickname from being an expert with antique weapons. He harvested a deer every year using his flintlock rifle. He didn't really want to be a part of the militia, but they did do a lot of outdoor things which he enjoyed. Violence was not a part of his nature. He was well liked by everyone who knew him. Women often complimented him on his good looks, his sandy hair, his grayish green eyes and his rough masculinity. He was not a pretty boy by any means.

Somewhere along in life Earl Hazzard got the idea that the government was his enemy. He listened to the rabble rousing opinions offered by talk radio hosts every day and this idea was constantly reenforced in his mind. The government was taking away our freedoms and they were making serious inroads into the right to bear arms or as Earl often said, our "second amendment rights." He always talked about government as an enemy of the people, but deep inside he wished he had the means of becoming part of it. He needed guns, not to hunt and protect his home, he needed them in case the government began to take away more of our freedoms.

When the local congressional representative, Marcia Butler, first took office and was giving a speech in the state capital of Charleston, Earl and his group of sixteen followers make the trip and heckled Marcia Butler to the point where she cut short her planned speech. Earl was very keen on the second amendment, but he was not up to par on the first amendment which guaranteed freedom of speech and opinion.

Earl and Flint both worked for the Gas Company. Flint spent many hours collecting gas well charts for others to interpret, while Earl worked in an office as one of the interpreters. They were lucky to have jobs since West Virginia had one of the highest unemployment rates in the country. As Flint put it, "half the state receives some kind of government assistance and the other half pays taxes to support them."

At various times in their lives, both Earl and Flint were recipients of that assistance. As Earl said it, "too many people on food stamps, government should cut out all those social programs." It didn't seem to dawn on Earl that his family was the recipient of food stamps and free medical care when he was unemployed. The fact that his children still received a free lunch in school didn't seem to be part of the "socialism" that he and his band of followers were so against. Earl's lifestyle contradicted his actions and beliefs, but he couldn't make that connection. He was full of anger and he was able to transfer and share this anger with others.

Earl relished his role as leader of the small group of militia patriots. There might be as many as twenty five participants at any given meeting. The paid membership fluctuated between fourteen and twenty four throughout the year. The group called themselves the Mountaineer Militia and were held together by friendship and hunting.

The Mountaineer Militia had purchased a building that was part of the old Grange and here they drank beer, held monthly meetings, and practiced firing their weapons on a rifle and pistol range behind the building. They would invite speakers who had like-minded interests and they had some great discussions with these people. Earl was always frustrated when Flint engaged these speakers from the "other-point-of-view." Flint would say, "It is like religion, you have to acknowledge there are some things that don't add up, even though you keep on believing."

2. Mavis Kramer

It was almost sunset when Mavis Kramer walked into the home of Earl Hazzard without knocking. Earl's wife Mary was startled for a moment, but relaxed when she saw Mavis. They were good friends. The absence of knocking didn't seem to bother Mary, since she figured Mavis was too upset about her brother's death for formalities. Mavis had a right to be upset, considering her brother had committed an act of terror and was shot down by the police.

Mavis looked around. "Where is he?"

Mary sent her eldest son into the living room where the youngest son was engaged in a video game. She looked concerned, as well as nervous. "Earl's out and should be back within the hour. Why do you want to see him? Can I make you a cup of tea? Can I do anything for you? We are all sorry about your brother Fred. You must be terribly upset and sad losing a brother that way. Everyone is shocked." She repeated, "You must be terribly sad."

"I'm more upset than sad. I was depending on Fred for money. Taking care of a two-year old kid with no father is not an easy job. Can't get any money out of wild Billy, he spends it all on moonshine."

Mavis Kramer was twenty two years old and two years previously had given birth to a baby girl which she named Chloe. The father, Willis "Billy" Perkins wanted to marry her, but Mavis said she would have trouble raising the kid and didn't want to also be supporting a dead-beat father at the same time. They were both eighteen and just out of high school. She would raise the child on her

9

own.

      The mother of Billy Perkins, Mildred, agreed to take care of the child when Mavis had a job and also to help out with the rearing. Mavis appreciated Mildred's efforts. Mildred was happy to have a beautiful grandchild and hoped Mavis would give her the child to raise. Mavis was pleased to have someone to share the responsibility of child-rearing, but she wouldn't part with Chloe under any circumstances.

      Mavis had received the news of her brother's adventure via television. There was no name withheld pending notifying next of kin. She immediately called the capitol police and was informed that her brother had killed a person and wounded several others. The body of Fred would be held for some time and released when all official questions were answered.

      Mary wanted to know if Mavis had any indication of Fred's intentions. "That's what I want to ask Earl about. Fred was part of that militia group that Earl runs. Grown men, running around with guns, playing cowboys and Indians. What are they up to?"

      Earl came through the door at that moment and offered his condolences to Mavis. It was Earl's manner of sincerity that changed the expression of Mavis from one of hostility to one of tolerance. Earl was shorter than most kids his age while he was growing and this prompted him to learn to appease and compromise or the alternative of getting beat up in some confrontation. He was expert at sizing up a situation and taking command of it. He compensated for his short stature, five feet six inches, by using his intelligence and intuition to outwit most adversaries. He had expected Mavis to come to him and he was prepared for the meeting.

      The "captain" of the militia wondered why his wife hadn't offered Mavis a cup of coffee or a tumbler of whiskey. Mary said that Mavis had just arrived and she hadn't had a chance to offer hospitality. The quick statement was better than a complete discussion of what had transpired. She would get the coffee going immediately.

Earl motioned to chairs around the rectangular kitchen table and Mavis obliged by sitting in one of them. Earl took a seat opposite her. Mary put out a package of cookies, then went back to the coffee.

With a serious expression Earl offered, "We certainly were surprised when we heard about Fred's actions. None of the guys I talked to suspected he would go and do something like that."

Mavis reiterated that it was Earl's militia organization that set Fred to action. "He wouldn't do something like that unless he was prompted by your group. After every meeting he always talked about how the government was tramping on our rights and we should do something about it. He got those ideas from you Earl. You're always bad-mouthing the government. You and that national gun organization."

"I have to agree with you that we agree the government is trampling on our rights and taking away our freedoms with prohibitive laws and taxes. Fred must have been trying to express his feelings. Did he leave any note or message or anything like that?" Earl seemed to be thinking and wondering why there were no notes or messages from Fred to indicate his intent.

"Not that I know of. He wasn't good at writing, or thinking for that matter. I understand he raised his hands in surrender and the cop just off and shot him. I sure would like to just off and shoot that cop."

Earl knew that revenge was a powerful motive. Here was Mavis with, in his mind, a justifiable reason to seek some justice. Perhaps he could use Mavis in the future. He would cultivate that motive for revenge for all it was worth.

"That's the way I see it. Fred must have just got mad, had his pistol with him, and just started blasting. Flint thinks Fred was trying

11

to get Marcia Butler, but made a mistake in identification."

"Why would Fred want to shoot our representative. Her office helped our family get government assistance when we needed it. She got me money and food stamps which I am still getting."

"It probably goes a lot deeper than that. Marcia voted for the gun legislation that will outlaw automatic weapons. That must have got Fred's anger boiling. She also voted for regulating the coal industry and you know how our state depends on employment in the coal fields. Our group members do not like environmentalists. They are just another source of government interference in our lives."

Mavis seemed to accept those somewhat flimsy reasons for shooting someone. "Fred was upset about that environmental coal clean-up. But didn't the government provide the funds for that?"

"Probably, I'm not sure, but we simply got to get the government out of our lives."

"Maybe so, but I like the free birth control pills I'm receiving from the county. Not that I'm using them for their intended purpose."

"That's one of our problems. We are becoming so dependent on government that we don't take the initiative to take responsibility for our own welfare."

Mavis had an expression of serenity. "Well, although I love Chloe, I wouldn't have had her if the free birth control pills had been available at the time."

Earl could see that Mavis was in favor of government assistance and indeed appreciated it. He had to come up with some tactic that would get her back to reality, that is his reality, that the government was somehow our enemy. This was his main thrust to keep his band of followers loyal to his mission and to keep him in control of the group. Mostly they went along with anything Earl said as long as the firing range was kept in good order and the meetings featured cold beer and snacks.

The coffee mugs were distributed and sugar and cream were set in the center of the table. Earl and Mavis took time to get their coffee organized. Mary took a seat at the table and put a spoonful of sugar into her coffee.

"Well, Mavis, you said you would gun down the cop that shot Fred. Are you serious, or are you just talking."

"I don't know Earl. Fred did kill someone and wound a bunch of other people. I don't know how many at this time. The news on it was kind of sketchy. Looking from that angle, maybe he deserved to be shot."

"We here in the mountains like to see justice done, an eye-for-an-eye, so to speak. My family was in a feud for over a hundred years. We never let a killing of our own get by without retribution. We will get the cop that shot Fred, since he was our kin. I will guarantee you that much."

Mary broke into the conversation. "Won't the police come and interview Mavis? Probably interview all of us. Won't they be trying to determine what drove Fred to shoot someone?"

Earl took a long swig on his coffee. "They probably will and Mavis has no idea why Fred would do such a thing, so they won't get anywhere there." He looked at Mavis. "Don't mention that Flint gave Fred the ride to Charleston. No sense in dragging Flint into this."

"I didn't know Flint went to Charleston with Fred. If Flint had any idea about Fred's intent, I'm certain he would have talked Fred out of it. Flint's a great guy."

The captain realized he had let some kind of cat out of a bag.

13

"I'm not sure that Flint drove Fred to Charleston, since I haven't talked to Flint. Come to think of it, Jimmy Critchlow said that he was with Flint during the shooting and they didn't know it was Fred that had done it. Anyway, when the cops come to interrogate you, don't mention anyone from the hills if you can avoid it."

"Why do you use the word interrogate? That makes it sound suspicious."

"Maybe a bad choice of words, let's say question. They will have questions about Fred's friends and activities. They will try to determine a motive. Maybe, Fred wanted to commit suicide and just take someone with him. He did have a gun in his hand when the policeman shot him. He would have dropped the gun if he had any sense about him."

"Yeah," offered Mavis, "if he had any sense about him. I think Fred had two rifles, but I never knew him to have a pistol."

3. Flint and Mavis

Flint had found a half sheet of paper wedged in the back of the passenger seat of his pick-up truck. He read it. - *The government is the enemy of the people. Marcia Butler represents the government and so Marcia Butler is the enemy of the people. We, the people, have got to rise up against a government that is taking away our freedoms. This action of mine is the first step to freedom.*

Flint thought that the concept and the language was a little too complicated to have been written by Fred. There was no doubt in his mind who had written it. The message could probably be traced to the computer or printer of its origin. Rather than tear it up, he decided to take the paper to Earl Hazzard.

Earl held the paper and said there were fingerprints all over it now and if they gave it to the police their explanations would just invite suspicion and more questions. Earl didn't mention that when he printed out the message he had used gloves and handed it to Fred so the only fingerprints on the message would have been Fred's. He tried to think of still getting the message out under Fred's name, but there was no way he could do it at this time. He looked at Flint.

"Fred doesn't have a computer. Where could he have gotten this printed?"

There was no doubt in Flint's mind where it had been printed. "Police have a way of getting erased messages off of computers. Maybe, Fred printed it up at the library."

"Come to think of it, Fred did ask to use my computer about a week ago. Maybe, he printed it up on my equipment. I wasn't with him when he used it so I don't know what he was doing."

Yeah-Earl. Flint nodded as if accepting the explanation. This seemed to satisfy Earl. There was a lot of other material hidden in the modem of the computer that would be embarrassing if exposed. Earl didn't think it through, but if push came to shove he would say that Fred often used his computer.

Earl was used to expressing false emotions with conviction. He looked at Flint with eyes almost brimming with tears. "I feel sorry for sister Mavis. Now she is alone in that dilapidated house with a baby to care for. You would think Fred would have thought of that."

Flint would go along with this line of thought. "Well, Fred did not seem to think things through. I suppose Mavis will be on public assistance now more than ever. Mildred will probably help her out and might even invite them to live with her. Now that Mavis has Fred's car, she might be able to get a part-time job somewhere."

"Yeah," said Earl, "that would be a good solution to our

15

problem."

It never occurred to Flint that Mavis was "our problem." Hill country people were notorious for helping each other out in time of need, but there were limits to this aid. Mavis would just have to deal with the government that everyone in Fred's circle hated. Flint mused, "Good thing we have public assistance to help out."

Earl's eyes narrowed. "People have to be responsible for their own welfare. Our country is plunging further into debt every day and nobody seems to care. We got to get back to the ideals of Ronald Reagan.

"I don't know Earl. Reagan left the country with the biggest debt in the history of the country at that time."

"Dammit, Flint, you always come up with some argument that contradicts reality."

"Yeah, I should never let facts get in the way of clear thinking."

The statement went over Earl's head. For some reason he thought Flint was agreeing with him. Flint was a good member of the militia group and supported Earl for the leadership so Earl had no doubt that Flint shared his beliefs. It was true, Flint thought the government was going too far with spending and increasing taxes. The government should get its act together by decreasing spending. Then, he would think, half the people in West Virginia was getting public assistance in some manner and what would happen to them if the government stopped public assistance. Flint was in favor of changing the nature of the government, but how could it be done, short of revolution.

* * *

Flint went to the home of Mavis Kramer. He had a bag of tools that belonged to Fred. Although the gas company provided all the tools a

16

worker would need, some workers liked to have their own set of the most used tools on hand.

Flint and Fred had worked together for many years and Flint was probably one of Fred's best friends when it came down to it. Jimmy was probably the best friend. Flint was also a good friend of Fred's sister Mavis. He was the one who had given her transportation when she needed to get to the hospital and have her baby.

Mavis had seen Flint coming up the walk and opened the door for him. She had two year old Chloe balanced on her hip. "I guess that's Fred's stuff. Would you like some coffee?"

"Yer right Mavis, this is Fred's stuff. I can give you a good price on it if you want to sell it. And yes, I'll take you up on that offer of coffee."

"I'll have to think about selling the tools, I might be able to use them around here."

Chloe was now in a high chair crumbling up a packet of crackers that came with restaurant soup. Mavis and Flint sat across the kitchen table looking at each other before the serious conversation would be started. He really loved the cherub faced Mavis with her uncombed dishwater blonde hair and her blue eyes that looked like they were always glistening. He imagined kissing those puffy cheeks as he had often done when they embraced as they met when Flint came to pick up Fred for the militia meetings.

Flint looked around the kitchen. There was an electric stove, refrigerator, a table and four chairs.

The floor was covered with linoleum that showed a lot of wear. The walls were a light tan with streaks around the stove that defied removal. There was a small framed photo of a man and woman on the wall. The man was wearing a miner's helmet. The woman was in a floral print dress. Flint got up and looked closely at the photo. "Never noticed this picture before."

17

"I just put it up. That's mum and dad. Taken about a year before he was killed in the mine. As you know, mum died shortly after. Funny how when one married person dies, the other one follows rather quickly."

"Yeah, that's the way it goes." Flint went back to his seat at the table.

Mavis looked into the face of her child and pointed to Flint. "This is Flint, can you say Flint."

"Fint." She patted the child on the shoulder. "Very good Chloe."

Mavis had set out some home made bread with margarine and jelly. She cut a lump off the end of the loaf, smeared it with jelly and put it on the high chair tray.

"It's a good thing the house is paid for, shack that it is. I was thinking of moving the refrigerator out to the porch and making it a complete shack. Take the wheels off the car and put it up on blocks."

Flint smiled at her. "You seem to be holding up well. Have the authorities been around yet?"

"No, they probably haven't figured out how to get back here in the wilderness. I did get a phone call from Charleston asking questions and agreed to a third degree sometime soon. Not much I can tell them. What can you tell them, since they will be asking you about transporting Fred to Charleston?"

It was a stab in the dark. Mavis wasn't certain that Flint had driven Fred to Charleston, since Earl Hazzard effectively covered up his casual remark.

"I don't think I'll tell them I took Fred to Charleston unless I can't avoid it. He left some kind of crazy message about the government and Marcia Butler in my truck. I don't think he intended to leave it in the truck, but forgot to take it with him. I destroyed it."

"What did it say?"

"Something about revolution and getting rid of the present government."

"Isn't that what your militia group wants? I know that Earl Hazzard put Fred up to that, but there's no way to prove it, so I won't mention it to the police."

"Do you want to get revenge on the policeman who shot Fred?"

Mavis put another small piece of jellied bread on the high chair tray. Chloe scooped it up and added more jelly to her face.

"The policeman shot Fred and was justified in doing so. It was Earl Hazzard who killed Fred and I will get him for that. No, Flint, my anger is not with the cop who was doing his job, my anger is with Earl Hazzard who set Fred up, took advantage of his slow witted mind. You know, as well as I do, that Fred wasn't the sharpest tack in the box. He was a follower and not a leader, not even a bystander. I don't understand why a smart person like you messes with Earl and his group of followers."

"It's something to do. We get exercise on our maneuvers and we get a lot of political discussion that interests me."

"And you drink a lot of beer and moonshine."

"Yes we drink a lot of beer and moonshine. We do contribute to some worthy causes. We built a new foot bridge for Jim Critchlow's aunt, so she could get over the creek from the road."

"Yeah, that was a good deed. Boy Scout stuff. She's my aunt too."

Flint tried to be upbeat. "As a matter of fact, I was talking to Earl yesterday and he was wondering what kind of help he could give you and Chloe."

"With government assistance, we don't need a whole lot of help. Chloe's grandma Mildred is willing to take her off my hands any time I want, but I love that child, she is me." And *That Child* just threw a piece of her jelly bread on the floor. Mavis picked it up and put it on the tray. Chloe took a bite and threw it back on the floor. Mavis picked the remnant up, put it in her own mouth and washed it down with a swallow of coffee.

Flint smiled. "I guess we are from different generations. If a girl your age, when I was your age, got pregnant she would marry the father before the child was born."

"What are you, some old fogey, about what, thirteen years older than me, same as Fred. You're not old enough to be my father, so we are of the same generation, you at the top of it, and me at the bottom. I guess Fred was of a different generation, at least in his mind, and I guess you are too. At least in outlook. I said it once before and I'll say it again, if I married Billy, I would have two children to look after instead of one."

"Well, Mavis, you are beautiful and I might say, well built, and you probably could find a decent fellow to marry if you moved out of these hills and to Charleston or Parkersburg."

"I'm not interested in getting married, though I do miss sex, even though my experience is very, very limited. What do you do for sex? Your wife skipped town quite a while ago and a tough good looking guy like you must be itching."

It was getting too personal for Flint. He sipped his coffee. "There's a woman in Grafton that I met years ago. She's a couple of years older than me. She works in the county office there. Her husband abandoned her and their boy when the boy was less than ten years old. He is in the marines now and comes home when he gets a chance. Nice kid. You would like him. Maybe I can fix you up with him."

"So you're saying you have a girl friend in Grafton."

"No, not really, we have an understanding. I go over to her place on Saturday night. We go to a dance hall that has a band playing and we discuss life and drink beer. Sometimes, we just stay home and watch television. I stay over at her house and in the morning she fixes me pancakes and eggs and I kiss her goodbye and come back to my labors."

Mavis took Chloe out of the high chair and put her on the floor. She pulled a box of toy cars and trucks from the shelf over the refrigerator and put it beside Chloe who was now sitting on the floor. She turned to Flint. "Maybe, you would like to save gasoline and have you're weekly sex closer to home."

"Maybe, but I do enjoy the week ends in Grafton."

"Why don't you have sex with me Flint, no strings attached. It's been, so long since I had sex, I'm getting crazy. Those television programs don't help the cause much. All that sexual innuendo. I read a lot and when I read novels there is all sex and little story. Drives me up the wall sometimes."

Flint was eager for that option, but didn't know how to pursue it. "Like you said Mavis, or maybe I said, we are of different generations."

"Flint, I don't know much about sex. As I said, I have very limited experience. You'll have to teach me the moves, what to do, different positions, how to do it properly." Flint mumbled under his

21

breath that he must be dreaming.

"Oh hell Flint, old lady Harmon and the guy she just married are about thirty years apart. I'm not asking you to marry me. We could try it out sometime. Sometime soon, I hope."

"Mavis, don't get me wrong, I would love to have sex with you and you said you are on the pill. Wow, you could probably have any guy around here you want."

"And for the time being, I want you. We can grow into each other. I'm sure of it. I have been thinking about this for some time now. It isn't just some spur of the moment thing, even though it might sound like it. You are the logical person for me. You have no attachments."

"Do you want to wait until you talked to the police?"

"No, I don't, right now doesn't seem to be a good time. How about tomorrow night around eleven, Chloe goes to bed at nine and she doesn't get up until five or six the next day."

"That would be fine." Flint was understating his opinion by a wide margin.

Mavis looked at Chloe. "Now that Fred's room is available I will move Chloe in there and have my own bedroom to do what I wish. Hint. Hint. I'll wait until the police have gone through Fred's things and given me an okay."

Flint rose from his chair. "I'll be leaving now, but I'll be back at eleven tomorrow night." He walked to the door. Mavis followed him. Chloe followed Mavis. Flint held Mavis by the shoulders and gave her a little kiss on the cheek. She returned the kiss to his lips.

When Flint stood facing Mavis he said he hadn't noticed her height before. She must be five foot five at least. She said, "Five foot six to be exact. When I had Chloe I was five foot four and believe it or not I grew two inches in height since then.

Mavis pulled Flint's face toward her and kissed him on the mouth again. "See you tomorrow."

He would have liked to continue the holding and kissing, but felt he didn't want to come off as some country bumpkin. "Until tomorrow then." Chloe smeared jelly on Flint's pant leg.

4. Corporal Charlie Fitch

It was two in the afternoon when there was a knock on the door of the Kramer home. Mavis opened the door to see two uniformed policemen standing there, a man and a woman. "I was expecting you, what took you so long?" She noticed the woman had a large brown envelope under her arm.

The woman spoke. "I'm sergeant Brenda Morgan and this is Corporal Charles Fitch. I guess you know why we are here."

"Yeah, come on in and have some coffee."

The pair entered the kitchen. Mavis waved them to a seat at the table. "This kitchen is where I live, maybe you would prefer we talk in the living room. I can set up the coffee there."

Sergeant Brenda Morgan said that the kitchen would be fine. Mavis told them that her daughter Chloe was taking a nap. She was a hard sleeper so they wouldn't be waking her. Chloe woke up when she felt like it. Both officers removed their hats. Mavis indicated a hat rack on the wall near the door then told them it would be okay to keep their hats on. They both put their hats back on. She looked at the cops and wished that she was one of them.

Sergeant Brenda was about thirty years old. Her breasts made a bulge in her tan shirt that was difficult to ignore. Her brown eyes and pleasant expression sparkled friendship. Some people seemed to be born with a pleasant expression that gave them an advantage in life.

Corporal Fitch was about six feet tall with an athletic build. He started the conversation by saying that he was born and raised in these parts, just over the hill at West Union. His mother still lived there. Mavis said that she had been there many times and the small restaurant there had rabbit on the menu. She laughed and said it was probably road kill. Fitch said he often ate road kill if he could get it while it was still fresh. Officer Brenda rolled her eyes. The conversation was getting too personal.

Mavis put out three cups, three spoons and a small container of cream. She moved the sugar bowl which was already on the table toward the officers.

"I really can't tell you anything why Fred would do such a thing. I didn't even know he had a hand gun. I don't believe the gun was his. His hunting rifle is in his room. Might be two rifles there, but I think he could only afford one. I don't touch his things, I only run the sweeper in there."

Apparently Officer Brenda would do the questioning and Officer Fitch was there for security insurance since the state had many incidents and lawsuits involving single interrogators. Officer Brenda said the gun Fred had was part of an arsenal stolen from a gun shop in Parkersburg. If Fred didn't own a gun, who could have given it to him? Mavis immediately thought of Earl Hazzard, but tried to be nonchalant. She lifted her shoulders and tightened her mouth to indicate "search me."

Mavis noticed Officer Charles Fitch looking at her with wonder in his eyes. His gaze certainly had more intent than normal police work. When their eyes met, she saw the intensity in his and smiled. The exchange didn't get past Officer Brenda who mentioned something about being on duty here and getting the preliminaries completed. Brenda tapped Fitch on the chest pocket. This prompted him to take out a note pad and pen from his shirt and begin writing.

"Fred's bedroom is in the back of the house. You can go through it if you like, you have my permission and don't need a search warrant."

Officer Brenda said they might just do that and they appreciated her cooperation more than she could imagine. Most people are hostile to the police and since Fred had been killed by a policeman they expected extreme hostility from his sister.

"No, if the events were as described, Fred should have been shot. He probably would have been executed anyway. After all, he did murder somebody. I'm sort of angry with him for leaving me when we depended on his job to keep us afloat."

Officer Fitch said that was a sensible attitude to take. Officer Brenda gave Fitch a look as if to say shut up and let me do the talking. Fitch was looking deep into the face of Mavis when he spoke. Officer Brenda was annoyed and with stern expressions let Fitch know she was annoyed. She told Fitch to check out Fred's room and see if anything unusual turned up. Mavis led Fitch to the room and their bodies pressed pleasantly together as she went back to the kitchen and Officer Brenda.

Fitch looked about the room that had limited light from a window with curtains drawn. He went to the window and pulled the curtains back. Where to start his search. There was some literature on a night stand beside the bed as well as a lamp. He looked at the literature. One was a plea from the NRA for extra donations because the Supreme Court was about to be packed with anti-gun justices. The other piece was from the secretary of the Mountaineer Militia about a meeting to discuss maneuvers.

A search of the room revealed nothing out of the ordinary. There was a closet with a business suit, several pairs of trousers, some shirts, mostly work shirts. On the floor of the closet were articles of clothing as if Fred changed into and out of them without bothering to hang them up.

Fitch went over to the chest of drawers, opened each one and plunged his hand into the socks, underwear, T shirts and other articles of cloth such as bandanas contained there. Nothing unusual. However, all was very orderly and clean. Fitch was impressed with the fact that the sock drawer was neater than his ever was.

There was a two space gun rack on the wall containing a rifle on the top rack. A small sack of shells hung from one of the other tines of the rack. Fitch went back to the closet to see if he had missed a rifle standing up in it. No rifle in the closet.

Fitch took the two pieces of literature and went back to the kitchen where Officer Brenda was writing on her note pad. Brenda looked up and raised her eyebrows. Fitch said there was nothing out of the ordinary, but the papers he held might be of interest to Brenda.

Brenda took the papers and looked at them, then turned to Mavis. "What is this Mountaineer Militia?"

"Oh, it's some kind of gun group that has meetings to pass the time. They have a small building up on the knob and they drink beer there and get into arguments."

It was only a short time before Officer Brenda learned that Earl Hazzard was the man who ran the Mountaineer Militia. She duly noted his name and the location of his house on her note pad.

Jimmy Crtichlow went to Charleston and officially identified the body of Fred. Officer Brenda didn't mention this to Mavis, but it saved Mavis a trip. Where did Mavis want the body deposited. As the only living relative they could find, it was her responsibility. Mavis had thought about that. A funeral would cost about five thousand dollars. Cremation would be close to two thousand. She didn't have that kind of money. What would happen if she didn't accept the body? Officer Brenda said it would be cremated and the ashes sprinkled on a bed of flowers planted every spring at the state capital. Mavis thought that was the route to go and it wouldn't cost her anything. There was no need to have a funeral. It wasn't Fred anymore since the spirit had left the body.

Officer Fitch broke into that conversation and said the university at Morgantown had a medical school and he was informed

26

that they would pay around a thousand dollars for any body donated to them. After the body was used for medical purposes the university would cremate the body and give the relative the ashes if they wanted them. Mavis liked that idea, especially the thousand dollars that came with it. She asked Officer Fitch if he would check it out and make the arrangements. Fitch said he would. Officer Brenda said they weren't in the advisement business and Fitch should just leave it up to Mavis. Fitch said he would do it on his off duty hours if that would please Brenda. Although they were friends, this exchange indicated a small measure of friction between them.

Officer Brenda indicated she was pleased with the cooperation of Mavis and others in the community and if Fitch wanted to, he could go out to the police car and call the university and check out the details needed. She would continue her talk with Mavis who was filling the cups with more coffee.

Officer Fitch went outside, taking his fresh mug of coffee with him. Officer Brenda Morgan unclasped the large envelope and removed a set of photographs. She moved them toward Mavis. "We don't know how your brother got to Charleston. Do you know?"

Mavis shook her head to indicate no, she did not know."

"Well, look at these photographs taken around the crowd at the gathering and see if you recognize anyone."

Mavis looked and saw the images of George "Flint" Haloway and Jimmy Critchlow standing under a tree. She passed that photo to the side and scanned each of the twelve in turn. "No, I don't recognize anybody."

The officer went back to photo number two. It was the one with Flint and Jimmy beside each other. Brenda put the back of her pen on the face of Critchlow and then moved it to Flint. "How about these guys?" Mavis knew that somehow Brenda knew, so there was no use in lying.

"They look like guys named Critchlow and Haloway, but I'm not sure. The photo isn't very clear to me. If you know who they are, why are you asking me?"

Officer Brenda said she was testing Mavis to see if she would cooperate. She knew that Haloway had visited her yesterday afternoon. Mavis said it was a poor photo and how did Brenda know she had been visited by Flint Haloway. "A neighbor said so."

"Which neighbor?" "We cannot divulge our sources."

The sparkling green eyes of Mavis lost their sparkle and took on a hostile aura. "Okay then, get out of here. This interview is over."

Officer Fitch came back in the house without knocking. "The university will gladly take the body and they will send a person to you with papers to sign. They asked when it would be convenient and I told them any time tomorrow. I hope that is okay with you. If that isn't, I'm supposed to call them back Maybe you want a last look at the body before they take it."

"No, I don't want to see him with a hole in his forehead. I'll remember him as he was."

Brenda said she was going to the car. As Brenda stood ready to exit the door, Mavis said if the police got all their news from the neighbors, there was no need for her to come back to this house. Officer Fitch wondered what that was all about. He would very much like to come back to this house.

Mavis looked at Charlie Fitch and said that his solution to her problem was great and she appreciated the effort he had made on her behalf and she couldn't thank him enough. Fitch looked into her face. His had the expression of wonderment. He said he might drop around the next time they are in the area and see how this worked out. Mavis indicated it would be fine with her. She looked into his face, smiled and pursed her lips. Brenda had already taken a seat in the police car.

When Fitch got into the car he asked Brenda why a warm interview turned into a cold one. Brenda said she screwed up and told Mavis a neighbor mentioned seeing Haloway visiting her house. When I wouldn't divulge the neighbor's name, she terminated the interview. "I can't blame her."

Fitch agreed that it was an unfortunate circumstance. He was hoping to keep their relationship with the natives on a cooperative basis even though he knew the hill people were fiercely loyal to each other, since he was one of them. "There are only about a dozen houses in this patch and I'm sure everyone is related somehow and knows each other's business."

There were houses scattered all along the main road that was on a ridge paralleling Route 50. Wherever the hill leveled off a cluster of houses existed. Each little cluster had a nick-name. If a stranger was looking for the Kramer residence he would be told to go over to Buckeye. If he was looking for the Hazzard residence it was Chestnut, the Crtichlow residence was at Oak Blight. Flint Haloway lived in Buckeye, just around a turn in the gravel and dirt road from Mavis Kramer.

Brenda Morgan looked at Officer Charles Fitch. "Something else happened in there Charlie, you looked like a love-smitten rooster."

"I don't know what it is, but she is the most beautiful woman I have ever seen, her voice, her eyes, her body. Crazy. Can't understand it. I seem to be trembling inside."

Brenda started the motor. "First impression Charlie. Fatal attraction."

It was eleven o'clock in the evening when Flint knocked on the door. Mavis answered. She was dressed in a skirt and blouse, rather than her usual jeans. She closed the door behind Flint and moved into him, took him by the head, pulled him down and gave him a kiss on the lips. She raced her tongue quickly over his lips before she withdrew the kiss. "That's to get us started." Flint assured her he had already started hours before he walked up the path to her kitchen door. He had thought about her almost every waking minute.

And, it was only a matter of minutes before they were in bed and consummating the agreement. Flint continued to feel her body as he continued his action with affection. Funny thing happened to Mavis. She kept getting this image of Officer Charlie Fitch, off and on, as she enjoyed the episode.

After the event, they each went to the bathroom in turn to wash up. Rather than continue the after-play they had engaged in, they dressed and went to the living room and sat on the sofa. Mavis asked if Flint wanted anything to drink. He said he would like a glass of the wine that he had brought with him or from the bottle he noticed on the kitchen sink when he came in. Mavis said she would like that also. She would save Flint's wine and serve him some of Mildred's home made stuff.

When the wine was served on the coffee table Mavis said, "Well, what do you think?" It was obvious to Flint what she was asking. He said it was tremendous and he hoped this was not going to be a one night stand. Mavis said she would be available whenever Flint was ready. Maybe they could set a regular meeting date, like, say Wednesday or Thursday nights. If things go well then maybe there would be in-betweens.

Mavis laughed. But, it was a hollow laugh. "I wouldn't want to interfere with your trips to Grafton." Flint didn't respond to that statement but said that Mavis could get grandma Mildred to watch Chloe and they could go dancing some Friday over in West Union. Mavis liked that idea, she needed to get out.

A sleepy eyed Chloe came into the living room. She lunged about. Mavis rose and led Chloe over to the sofa and laid her out where she had been sitting. Flint moved to the big stuffed easy chair that had an adjustable handle. He finished his wine and set the glass on the coffee table.

Before the conversation could continue Chloe rose from the sofa and went over to Flint, said "Fint" and crawled up on his lap, put her head against his chest and appeared to go to sleep. Mavis went to extract her. Flint raised his hand. "No, let her sleep. Maybe get a blanket to cover her."

Mavis came back with a small blanket and put it over Chloe. Flint used the chair lever and moved the back of the chair to a slant. He kicked off his shoes. Mavis went to the bedroom, came back with a blanket, kicked off her shoes, lay on the sofa and covered herself with the blanket. Soon there were three sleeping bodies in the living room.

5. Earl's Philosophy

The natives of West Virginia are a people proud of their heritage and their state. Except for the large cities, they identify themselves by counties. They are a homogeneous group descended from the old Scotch-Irish line. They are proud of their state motto *Montani Semper Liberi* and they wear it as a badge. The state has the lowest percentage of foreign born immigrants in the country, one percent. Unfortunately, the state ranks among the top in prejudice scales. Usually, outsiders entering the hills are regarded with suspicion, even by the most enlightened of residents.

Earl Hazzard had agreed to meet with the police at his home concerning the action of Fred Kramer. He had taken the day off from work. It would be an informal meeting, just to get some idea on the movements of Fred before the event. He was assured everything said would be off-the-record. Earl's wife Mary said she would go to the shopping mall for the afternoon. The boys would be in school, so there would be no interference from family members.

31

Earl saw the police car park on the road in front of his house and went out on the porch to greet Officer Charles Fitch who was walking up the path from the parking area. They exchanged introductions. Earl said he was hoping to talk to that lady cop with the big boobs. Charlie Fitch didn't laugh, but shook his head. "She's off today."

Earl's house was a step above most of the houses in the patch. It had attractive tan aluminum siding on its two story frame. The roof was of brown sheet metal which appeared to be a part of the huge oak trees surrounding it. A cement walkway led from the parking area to the front porch.

Inside was a modern kitchen on the ground floor along with a living room and a den. Earl showed Officer Charlie around. He didn't have to explain the water and septic systems, since Charlie had been raised under those conditions.

Earl said they could sit in the den where he already had a fifth of bourbon and some tumblers ready for the meeting. The den had a small leather upholstered sofa and matching chair. A coffee table in front of the sofa was perfect for watching television. On one side of the room was a large gun display case with four rifles and two handguns in it. A trophy deer head was mounted over the gun case.

Earl pointed to the head. "Got that fellow just over the hill from here, twelve points, went into the record books of West Virginia, as well as Boone and Crockett."

"Nice rack. I used to like hunting when I was a kid. I hunted your hollow a couple of times. Deer seemed to be a lot smaller ten years ago. Haven't had much time to hunt these last few years. I'll get back to it once I get settled."

Earl motioned for Charlie to take a seat at the sofa which he did. Earl sat in the chair. Charlie noticed the chair seat was about three inches higher than the sofa. He had read somewhere that this was a technique used by executives to give them a way of talking down to employees. Usually, when this occurred he would say he preferred to stand and thus thwart the attempt at dominance. He figured he would stand if the situation warranted it.

"Nice gun closet you got there Earl. Looks expensive."

"Yeah, it's expensive, but it's practical. All those guns are cleaned and ready to go."

"Go where Earl?"

Earl was taken off guard by the question. He couldn't think of a good response. He settled for "Go wherever, they are needed."

"Where could they possibly be needed?"

Earl said that you never know when a person would have to defend his family and property. The NRA believes everyone should have the right to defend family and property. "

"Everyone believes that a person has the right to defend family and property and to use force if necessary, Earl. You couldn't find any normal person in the country who believes otherwise."

Earl took on his pontifical demeanor. "When the stuff hits the fan in Washington DC, the people in that area will be abandoning the area like rats. Where are they going to go? The only place is west and Route 50. That will take them right through our area and they will be in gangs foraging, looting and only God knows what else. Well, we will be ready for them."

Charlie tried to be friendly. "Yeah, I hear you. But that seems likely never to happen in your lifetime. Besides, we have law enforcement to prevent that."

Earl poured a shot of whiskey into a tumbler and swallowed it with one gulp. "If the government outlaws guns, then only outlaws will have guns."

"Good bumper sticker Earl. That might be a good thing. If only outlaws had guns then the police will be able to identify them and lock them up. The way it is with guns now, we don't know how to separate the good guys from the bad guys. Lots of shootings lately, people getting killed for no reason."

Earl smiled. "Here's another bumper sticker for you. Guns don't kill people, people kill people."

Charlie said he agreed with that except he would modify the bumper sticker to read - Guns don't kill people, people with guns kill people." He went on to say that limiting guns to the home and hunting would make law enforcement easier. No need to have weapons that fire 30 shots a second in the hands of civilians. "That would sure tear up a deer."

"Hate to tell you this officer, but we haven't had much luck with law enforcement around here. Many burglaries and other crimes left unsolved."

Fitch thought this was a good lead in. "Is this why you formed the Mountaineer Militia? So when the stuff hits the fan, you guys will be able to protect these hills."

"You got it." Earl was happy to have Officer Charles Fitch explain it in that manner. Now he wouldn't have to defend his organization of the militia.

"Was Fred Kramer a member of your militia?"

Earl used the term "sort of." Fred wasn't a serious member. He had some kind of grievance against the government. He attended meetings infrequently, and when he did, he was always a distraction with tirades against the government taking away our basic freedoms.

"They do take away our freedoms, reckless spending is one of them, you know, spends our tax money on frivolous things like Cowboy Poetry gatherings."

Charlie agreed that there were questionable expenditures of government at every level. However, he was glad to have the job with the state and its retirement system. He pressed Earl again on the use of police and national guard in handling disasters and mob situations. Earl said that this was true and a needed expense, but when the police and national guard were not around it was necessary for the citizens to take action.

This gave Charlie a lead in to action against the government. "Do you believe that if the government doesn't meet your needs, you have a responsibility to take action against the government?"

"Absolutely, we have to protect the constitution and when the government violates this sacred document we have to do something about it."

"Like shoot a member of the house of representatives."

Earl took a swig right from the bottle. "Maybe that's what Fred Kramer had in mind when he went to Charleston. I figure he must have wanted to shoot Marcia Butler. He had often complained about her environmental preachings. You know she was an enemy of coal and we in the hills rely on coal for our livelihood."

Charlie said he agreed that Fred meant to shoot Marcia Butler, but he shot the wrong person. Well, shooting anybody is wrong. Also, he didn't believe there was a war on coal. Most of the people in this area worked in schools, gas, electric, and timber. Earl countered with the idea that most of the people in this area were on government hand-outs and that has got to stop. Charlie didn't want to get into that bag of worms.

They both agreed that Fred intended to shoot Marcia Butler, but had made a mistake. Charlie wanted to know how Fred got to

Charleston. He knew that George Haloway had taken Fred there, but he wanted to hear it from Earl. Of course, Earl pleaded ignorance of the matter.

Where did Fred get the handgun? It was Earl's opinion that the gun was probably purchased at the annual gun show in Parkersburg. His group went to at least one day of the show and many of them made purchases there. Charlie didn't mention that the gun Fred used was a weapon stolen from a gun shop a few years ago. He wanted to see if Earl would tip his hand. Earl didn't.

The meeting had reached its conclusion and Officer Fitch rose to leave and thanked Earl for his candid expressions and views, not only on Fred, but on society in general. Earl believed he had led the young officer to his way of thinking. Charlie went over to the deer mount and pretended to examine it carefully and made some comments on the expertise of the mount. Earl stood behind him and said it was done by a man over at Melbourne. People came from all over the state for his services.

Charlie said he grew up in West Union, so he knew Melbourne and the area very well. What Charlie was actually doing was taking a mental note on the rifles and handguns in the case below the mount. When he got back to his car he would write this information on his notepad and see if it matched any of the weapons stolen in the gun shop heist. He didn't expect stolen weapons to be on display, but he would record what he saw anyway.

* * *

George "Flint" Haloway agreed to give a statement to the police at the town hall in Salem. He would take off work on Tuesday afternoon. When he arrived at the town hall, he was met by Sergeant Brenda Morgan and Corporal Charles Fitch. Introductions were made and the trio settled at the table in the meeting room. There was a stenographer in attendance.

Flint said he was going to Charleston to get feed for his livestock of six sheep and a steer. He also had to drop off two sheep at the feed store that would be picked up by their new owner on

Monday. When he mentioned it to Fred at work, the man said that if Flint would go on Saturday he would ride along with him. Fred and Flint both worked for the gas company. They repaired valves and read pressure gauges and did an assortment of other duties. They worked alone, but would see each other just about every working day when they went to the shed to pick up special tools, punch out and record what they had done.

Brenda Morgan kept smiling at Flint. Why not? Flint was a well built, clean shaven, very masculine fellow with light brown hair that hung over to the left side of his head in a half curl. He sat and walked upright, no stooping shoulders or head bent down.

Of course, Flint said he didn't know what Fred was about to do. Fred said he heard that Marcia Butler was going to speak at a rally in Charleston and he wanted to hear what she had to say. Marcia was not very popular with the hill people. She was elected mostly on the vote of the city and town folk.

"I told Fred that I didn't like the idea of waiting around a couple of hours while the festivities were going on. I had to get back, since I had an appointment on Saturday evening. He said that I could go on back home and he would catch the bus. Well, after I dropped off the sheep and got the feed loaded and did some banking, the bank closed at noon, I ran into Jimmy Critchlow. We got to talking and I mentioned that Fred was going to a rally that featured Marcia Butler. Jimmy said he would like to hear what she had to say and he had a few questions he would like her to answer. I said he should write her a letter rather than shout out. Anyway, I thought okay, I'll go along with it, find Fred and tell him I'll give him a ride back and he didn't have to catch the bus. I have a regular meeting in Grafton every Saturday, so I was anxious to get back."

Brenda wanted to know if Fred ever expressed anti-government feelings. No - he didn't seem to have that kind of mindset. Did Fred ever express hate for Marcia Butler? No - I don't ever recall him expressing that opinion. "None of us thought much of Marcia Butler and her environmental policies that would affect our

37

livelihood. But, certainly not enough to assassinate her."

Officer Charles Fitch had a note pad in front of him. He noted that Flint said Fred had no strong political feelings. He would contrast that with the statement of Earl Hazzard which was that Fred was a very vocal anti-government agitator.

"No one thought strongly about it, except maybe Fred. Why did you use the term assassinate?" Officer Brenda had moved her eyebrows up slightly, accentuating her question.

Flint hunched up his shoulders and relaxed them. "I guess if you shoot a public official it is assassination, if you shoot Joe Blow that is simple murder."

Have any idea where Fred got the handgun he was using? No, all the hill people have long guns and almost everyone, including most of the women, are hunters. "I never owned a handgun, but I have used many of them in target practice."

Brenda didn't mention that the handgun was among items stolen from a gun shop in Parkersburg. She regretted mentioning that to Mavis and hoped Mavis didn't catch that. She didn't want to tip anyone off that the investigation at this time had shifted from the shooting of the committee woman to an investigation of the stolen hand gun. Most of the present investigation of Fred's actions was to try to trace the handgun.

For all practical purposes the case against Fred Kramer was closed except there were legal documents that had to be prepared. Brenda said it would only take a few moments for the stenographer to get the statement of Flint into an acceptable form, Flint could sign it and the matter would be closed. Officer Brenda Morgan held out her hand. Flint took it. Brenda held it longer than usual. She smiled at Flint. "You have a beautiful strong hand. Very masculine. I like that in a man." Flint felt a glow of warmth creep over him. Too bad, he already had a deal with Mavis.

There only seemed to be one restaurant in the town of Salem. So Flint went there and sat at a table that looked out on a small public square. He asked the waitress if this was the only restaurant in town. She said there was a college at the other end of town and they had a cafeteria that was open to the public. Actually, their breakfast was cheaper than here, "but, we beat them on lunch and supper."

Soon Officers Morgan and Fitch came into the restaurant. Flint waved them over to his table. "Where's the stenographer."

Charlie Fitch answered. "She is a local woman and went home as soon as she could get away from us."

There was a feeling of friendship among the three diners. Brenda kept looking at Flint as if he was a prize steer at the farm show. She inquired about his marital status and he said as far as he knew he was still married although his wife Marjorie had taken off around six years ago and was somewhere in Florida. "No need to dwell on it. Don't miss her at all. I have a lady friend who takes care of all my needs."

Corporal Charles Fitch sat up straighter. "You mean, Mavis Kramer." Both Brenda and Flint noticed a sense of panic in his voice. Flint smiled.

"No, not Mavis, we are a generation apart. Someone more my own age. When your informer said they saw me going to the Kramer house it was to take Fred's tools to Mavis. That was the first time I ever set foot in that house. Now that Fred's gone, Mavis will need more help from the community."

Charlie made a grim mouth, then relaxed. "Just out of curiosity, is Mavis hooked up with anybody. I know the father of her baby isn't with her. I looked up the court records."

39

"Why would you do that?" asked Flint. "She has nothing to do with the shooting except to be a sister of the shooter."

Brenda broke in with a laugh. "Poor Charlie, he got one look at Mavis and he was hooked. He said she dances in his mind and he can't concentrate on important things. That is sickening, but very romantic."

Flint laughed and looked at Brenda. "Maybe Mavis is important things to Charlie. She probably has no reciprocation in that direction." At least, he hoped so.

Actually, Flint was wrong. Mavis thought of Charlie. She liked the sparkle in his light brown eyes. She liked his clean shaven face, his boyish looks. She hoped Charlie would not disappear from her life. She feared that any association with any man in the future would be jeopardized by Chloe. However, Chloe was more important to her than any man could ever be. But, she thought about Officer Charlie Fitch a lot after first meeting him.

Charlie said that he thought he might drop around to see Mavis. He would use the excuse that he wanted to know how she made out with the university and the disposal of Fred's remains. What did Flint think of that approach?

"I did see Mavis after the medical university man showed up with the papers. She was very grateful for your help in that matter."

"Yeah," laughed Brenda, "she owes you one."

Charlie was serious. "Oh, she doesn't owe me anything. I would never use my position to any advantage." He turned to Flint. "Could you drop a hint to Mavis that I'm interested in her. Be subtle, like, say, Charlie Fitch did a lot of talking about you when we had lunch in Salem."

Flint smiled and said he hated to get mixed up in any

romance, Charlie would have to pursue that avenue on his own. Of course, he now had his own selfish motives. Mavis was probably the best sex he ever had in his life. Their affair had just begun and he would really - really hate to see it end so soon. He already had a love for her and he didn't know how far it would go. He adored little Chloe and loved having her little cheek press against his. Her little kisses had an angelic quality about them.

"Well, anyway," said Brenda, "we are not through with the investigation because we don't know where Fred got the gun. It wasn't registered and we couldn't find a paper trail leading to where it was purchased." She thought Flint would have an opinion on it.

Flint was at a loss to come up with an opinion. Deep inside, he suspected that Earl Hazzard have given Fred the hand gun, but he couldn't prove it. He assured Brenda he had no idea Fred was carrying a gun when they went to Charleston. He had never seen Fred with a hand gun. When they practiced shooting at the Militia range Fred never used a hand gun. Of course, Flint was not at the practice range all the time.

They exchanged biographies. Brenda and Charlie were both graduates of the West Virginia Police Academy. Both were college graduates. Charlie had grown up in the small town of West Union, only twenty miles from Salem, so he knew the area very well. Brenda was a city girl and had spent her life in Charleston when she wasn't in the academy. She was thirty years old and had a cousin who was also in law enforcement. How about Flint?

To their surprise, Flint said he had a degree in forestry and was waiting for one of the ancient forest supervisors to die and hoped he would get the job. West Virginia had a dozen state forests and there was also a segment of federally owned forest. The gas company job paid well and it was in the environment that suited him so if the forest job opened up the competition for it would be great, probably political, and he always had the gas company job to fall back on.

One of the things that impressed Brenda was the number of

hill country people that had college degrees. Flint assured her, "We might be hill billies, but we're not hicks." He added, "You flatlanders live in your own world of prejudices." He gave a slight laugh and so did Brenda and Charlie.

6 Militia Meeting

A guest speaker was scheduled at the clubhouse for Wednesday evening. It was Ray Pflipps of Radio KUKV located in Tennessee. Earl Hazzard had put pressure on all members to attend. The topic would be the Ruby Ridge shoot-out and other related events.

The meeting was well attended by thirty four men and six women who were wives of some of the men. The small meeting room was packed. Seating was at a premium and some of the guys got planks and cement blocks from outside and made temporary seating against the back wall.

Earl Hazzard was in his glory as he made small talk with Ray Pflipps and introduced him to members standing within ear shot. There was no podium but there was a desk that Earl and the speaker could sit behind which would give the meeting a more formal atmosphere.

Ray Pflipps was a rotund man with a grinning, pious expression. His black hair mottled with gray had thinned considerably and he combed what was left of it from left to right. He wore a dark gray business suit. His eyes seemed to shine from within rather from reflection. He held his head at an angle that gave the impression of a man who was jogging.

The gathering was called to order by Earl who said he hoped Mavis Kramer would be in attendance because he knew she would be interested in this topic. Flint was sitting in the back on one of the temporary seats. He laughed to himself.

"I would like to remind the members that we will be holding maneuvers on Sunday at two o'clock." He smiled at the joke he was about to tell. "That is two o'clock in the afternoon, of course." He asked the members to car pool and said they would assembly at the bottom of Camp Mistake Hill. "We will meet where the main road joins the old lumber road going up the knob."

Earl said he wished Mavis had decided to bury the body of Fred. Then they would have a shrine to remind them that their work against the excesses of government was just beginning. It was a work in progress in many areas of the government and the famous Ray Pflipps was invited to speak because he would inspire them further. Earl thought that maybe the members could come up with some funds and they could build a monument to Fred. He asked if anyone had an opinion on that.

Elmer Atkins rose to his feet. "I don't know what Fred was up to, but I don't think he did what he intended to do. I think he was after Marcia Butler, but he made a mistake. Fred was like that, never quite getting anything right. I don't think we should commemorate a guy who made a mistake and brought some infamy to our organization." He sat down to a murmur of affirmative sighs.

This nodding and affirmation was not lost on Earl. "At least Fred's intentions were in keeping with our philosophy and we should hold him in high esteem in our minds and hearts even if we do not erect some reminder of him. At this time I would ask you all to bow your heads in a minute of silence to contemplate the passing of our friend Fred Kramer."

Earl and Ray Pflipps bowed their heads. Many of the congregation did likewise. Flint was twitching his nose as he surveyed the bowed heads. Across the room Jimmy Critchlow, who hadn't bowed his head saw Flint looking around. Their eyes met and they nodded and smiled at each other. Flint remembered their puzzled conversation shortly after the shooting. They had concluded the event was simply bizarre. Flint had personal feelings about the event that he didn't relate to Jimmy. He wondered if he should have approached the police at that time and admitted he knew Fred and had given him a ride to Charleston. Silly, of course that's what he should have done, as well as give the police all the information on Fred so they wouldn't have to waste time getting it on their own.

The minute passed and Earl introduced the speaker Ray Pflipps as a great patriot, a renowned talk show host, and author of several books. He had asked Ray to bring along some books for sale and Ray agreed to autograph them if someone should so desire. Ray rose to his feet to a robust applause. Tonight's topic would be the Events at Ruby Ridge.

The guest speaker stood at the desk, looked around and smiled. "This is a nice turnout. Before I begin I would like to thank your commander for inviting me here. I would also like to thank Elmer and Alicia Atkins for boarding me during my stay in the area. Alicia makes the best chicken en dumplings I ever tasted. We have a mission here, mainly to get government off our backs and lower taxes. I know we need taxes to support the military, build the country's infrastructure of roads and bridges and regulate money, but that's about it. I don't want to stray too far from my topic, which is the events that occurred on Ruby Ridge which will illustrate the incompetence of government law enforcement. If the government can't do it, then we have to do it." This was echoed with a spattering of "hear hear."

The Ruby Ridge Incident according to Pflipps

Every person not connected with the federal government could come up with a logical reason to distrust and despise the government if they put their minds to it. The feds have proven time and again that they are perpetually victimizing the people. Native Americans were screwed at Wounded Knee. Japanese Americans were put in internment camps. African Americans had slavery. These are glaring, well publicized, examples of government betrayal of trust. These were crimes against ethnic and religious minorities. However,

44

this sense of disenfranchisement and oppression is no longer strictly the domain of ethnic or religious minorities. The incident at Ruby Ridge, which was followed by the incident at Waco has given rise to rage that decent people must express somehow. We will discuss the retaliation required at a later time. I am here to give you the facts about Ruby Ridge.

Randy and Vicki Weaver were just your average white supremacist couple trying to make their way in Iowa. After a string of lost jobs and a failed Amway franchise, they became convinced that the Zionist Occupation Government, that's what they called the U.S. Government, was about to launch an all-out war against its own citizens. So they spent $5,000 on a 20-acre parcel in Idaho and tried to raise a family beyond the clutches of the imminent New World Order.

If you're the anal-retentive type, you probably already know that there is no "Ruby Ridge" in Idaho. That's the government name for the area. The Weavers built their cabin out of scrap lumber on Caribou Ridge, near Ruby Creek, eight miles from the nearest settlement. They home schooled their kids and kept out of the mainstream of society. They put up signs such as White Power is Supreme. They made no bones about being white supremacists.

Randy began associating with committed white supremacists. In July 1986, Randy attended the World Congress of Aryan Nations at their headquarters near Hayden Lake. In all, he would attend at least three Aryan Nations functions during his time in Idaho.

At the 1996 World Congress he befriended an overweight biker by the name of Gus Magisono. In actuality, Magisono was an undercover ATF, Alcohol Tobacco and Firearms informant by the name of Kenneth Fadeley. Three years later, Gus asked Randy to sell him some sawed-off shotguns. Randy agreed. According to Fadeley, the guns were sawed off shorter than the legal minimum -- meaning, Randy had violated federal weapons laws. This was obvious entrapment, a favorite ploy of the feds.

Of course, even if the guns were exactly as the rat described, the whole setup reeks of entrapment. The ATF confronted Randy in

45

June 1990 and offered him the opportunity to be their eyes and ears in the Aryan Nations organization. Either that, or face hard time in a federal penitentiary for sawing off the shotguns. It was an offer he couldn't refuse.

Randy Weaver made a mistake, he refused to go along with the feds. He gave them the middle finger and related the offer to his white supremacist buddies.

The ATF realized they had made a mistake and organized for their next move. They arrested Randy Weaver in January 1991. They took him to the county jail, where he spent the night. The next day, Randy was brought before federal judge Stephen Ayers.

During the hearing, Judge Ayers told Randy that he would probably have to pay the government's court costs. Since Weaver had no financial assets this meant he would lose his property.

Randy should have had a lawyer. Even if he couldn't afford one, the government was obligated to provide one. Randy's wife Vicki mailed two letters to the U.S. Attorney's Office in Boise.

One was addressed to "The Queen of Babylon" and stated,
"

The other letter was addressed to "Servant of the Queen of Babylon, Maurice O. Ellsworth, U.S. Attorney.

Weaver failed to show up in court on February 20, so the judge declared him a federal fugitive. Seems simple enough. The problem was that the summons they received in January had the wrong date printed on it. It said he was to appear March 30, not February 20.

The family assumed that the feds were trying to humiliate Randy as an example to other potential informants. When the Weavers discovered that Randy was now officially classified a fugitive for no apparent reason, they turned paranoid and concluded that the government's goal was to assassinate him. So they hid out in the cabin for a year and a half, making few appearances in town, and keeping rifles close by.

46

The U.S. Marshals decided to mount a raid on the Weaver property. They knew that this would be difficult. The family lived in a remote, mountainous area. They kept rifles and knew how to use them. Randy was a former member of the Green Berets in the Army. So the feds opted for a military-style operation.

It was probably the single worst decision in the entire chain of events. The escalating tension on both sides could have been defused if the feds had only dispatched a plainclothes agent to the cabin accompanied by the local sheriff. It probably would have mitigated the Weavers' fears that the government was trying to kill Randy. Maybe he would have refused to accompany them back to jail, but the feds would have understood that the Weavers were at least willing to obey the law.

When the family noticed their dogs barking at something in the trees on the morning of August 21, 1992, they soon realized that the Zionist Occupation Government had finally launched a sneak attack. An armed reconnaissance team crept up to the cabin. When one of the dogs noticed them it began barking, so the feds shot it. By this time, the two boys in the household were already outside. Sammy Weaver shot at the intruders. We have a right to defend our property and family, don't we? Maybe so. One of the men returned fire and killed Sammy. Then Kevin Harris shot back at the commandos, killing U.S. Marshal William Degan. Suddenly, the firefight ended and both sides retreated.

Kevin returned to the cabin and the surviving Marshals carried their comrade's body back to base camp. Both groups would later claim they had acted in self-defense, and that the other was first to inflict death. In other words, both sides laid claim to the legal argument in *John Rambo* v. *United States Government*: "They drew first blood, not me! They drew first blood!"

Sadly, the creation of the Department of Homeland Security in the beginning of the 21st century gives some indication of the potential for abuses that far outweigh the ones committed by the ATF.

47

From the beginning, Randy insisted that he had never been a white supremacist willing to deny rights to other than white people. "I'm not a white supremacist. I'm a white separatist. I was born white. I can't help that. If I was black I'd probably be affiliated with a black group, but as it is, I don't belong to anything. I don't believe I'm superior to anyone, but I do believe I have the right to be with my own kind of people if I choose to."

We can say that this incident of the federal government versus Randy Weaver was a draw. Randy was convicted of a firearm violation. It appeared that there was nothing could be done about the death of the federal agent and the Weaver child.

Nowadays, Randy Weaver spends a lot of time on the gun-show circuit, although as a convicted felon he is ineligible to legally own a firearm. Weaver gives speeches and signs copies of his autobiography.

And he's become an atheist. Consequently, he no longer believes that God loves the white man most of all. Randy still thinks the races shouldn't mix, but there's no theological basis for it. It's just his personal opinion.

The incident at Ruby Ridge, let me remind you there is no place named Ruby Ridge in Idaho, the incident at Ruby Ridge (laughed) led to the incident at Waco, that the liberal press labeled Waco Whackos, but when you investigate that story you will realize they weren't so whacko.

Pflipps sat down to a hearty applause. He rose while the applause was still rolling. The applause ceased.

"If anyone has a question or comment, I will be happy to accept it. Please rise to let me know you wish to participate."

Billy Perkins rose. "Wouldn't all of this been avoided if Randy just gave up and went with the marshals."

Pflipps was still on his feet. "No, there was personal integrity involved. Weaver had been bushwhacked by the feds. He was encouraged to commit a crime. Up to then he had been a law abiding citizen, even if he didn't like some of the laws."

Floyd Maynard rose and Pflipps nodded toward him. "Billy,

how would you, or any of us, like it if you was being pushed around and back stabbed. There was an element of pride involved here. We got to stand on our two feet and fight, we might get knocked down, but, at least, we won't be on our knees." A short burst of applause followed. Flint Haloway and Jimmy Critchlow were not applauding. However, in his mind, Floyd Maynard thought he had made a good point.

7. Good and Bad News

It was a few minutes after midnight Wednesday evening. Mavis and Flint were sitting on the sofa in her living room. A half hour ago he was having sex with her and she was enjoying it immensely.

There were glasses of wine on the coffee table which both of them had been sipping. Mavis got on her knees on the sofa and gave Flint a prolonged kiss on the lips. "We sure feel like we belong together." Flint said that was true and he never felt closer to anyone in his life than he now felt to Mavis. She was delighted to hear that statement and kissed him again.

"You better cool it Mavis, I feel a surge coming on."

"Let it come, there is no law that says we have to limit ourselves to one a night."

Flint began to feel her body through her clothes. She was wearing her plaid skirt so she easily slipped her panties off and lay on her back. He was ready and more than willing and accepted the offer.

This was a prolonged event and both enjoyed the experience for its affection as well as its physical nature.

"I was worried that Chloe would wake and come in." said Flint.

"She sleeps well. Except for that first night you were here."

49

Flint said he had some bad news he had to share with Mavis. Of course, she became somewhat alarmed. "Your wife Marjorie is coming back after five years on the run."

"No, not that bad. It's bad news for me and probably good news for you."

It took a minute for what Flint had said to sink in. "Don't keep me in suspense."

Flint led up to what he was about to say by going through the events of his statement to the authorities. How he met with Troopers Brenda Morgan and Charles Fitch in the restaurant after the meeting. He said all Charlie Fitch talked about was Mavis. He could see a glow of excitement slowly creeping over her face.

"What did he say, come on, tell me."

"He said he couldn't get you out of his mind and asked me how he might get to know you better and if I thought you would give him a chance. He kept talking about your cute voice, your cute face, your cute body. Finally, Trooper Brenda said she was sick of hearing it and for Charlie to change the subject."

"You're putting me on Flint. I did cotton to the guy. I thought about him for a while and then just gave it up." Actually, she hadn't given it up and during the first session of the evening Trooper Charlie Fitch came to mind just before she climaxed.

Flint was serious. "He does seem like a nice level headed guy. He has a good income and even though he is a serious fellow, you could probably have some good times with him. I reminded him about Chloe and he said he saw Chloe as a miniature version of you and since he was smitten, his word, by you, he would be smitten by Chloe. She would not interfere with his honorable intentions, again, his words."

Mavis was getting more excited. Here was a clean cut well employed man only a few years older than she, interested in her. She had to fight off the local yokels, but she couldn't ignore this opportunity.

Flint curled his lips into his mouth. "Gawd, Mavis, I would hate to give you up."

"You wouldn't have to give me up for quite a while Flint. We will have our Wednesday nights together regardless of where the trail leads with Charlie. After all, you spend the weekends in Grafton with, what's her name, you never told me her name."

"Michelle."

"Oh that's a pretty name. Is she a pretty woman?"

"It's hard to tell, I've been with her so long, I never thought about it. Yeah, I guess you would say she is pretty. She has guys after her all the time also and she says she puts them off and I believe her."

"Any woman would be glad to have an affair with you Flint and as you have found out, I am one of them."

It was the following afternoon when Mavis saw Charlie Fitch, dressed in civvies, coming up her path toward the door. Chloe was taking her nap. Mavis decided to not rush to the door, but give Charlie some time to cool his heels. Charlie rapped on the door three times, waited, rapped three more times, waited and rapped again. Mavis bit her lower lip. She hadn't dressed for the occasion. She was in her usual blue jeans and white blouse covered with a pale blue sweater and a smear of Chloe's lunch. She thought her hair was a mess. It was a cool day at the end of September and she had the space heater plugged in.

51

Charlie rapped again. Mavis paused for a second then went to the door. "Officer Fitch, you are not in your uniform."

"Hi Mavis, sorry to bother you, but I wanted to find out how the disposition of the body turned out and if you got the money from the university that was promised."

"Please come in Officer."

The word Officer put Charlie in a state of panic. He wanted this to be informal and personal and the word Officer indicated some sort of formal put-off."

"Please, please, I beg you, call me Charlie. I didn't really come here to talk business. I confess, I used that as an excuse just to see you, be with you, and see if we could get to know each other better."

"I know Charlie. I know. Flint said he thought you would be coming around. I didn't expect you so soon and I'm a mess."

"You look beautiful to me."

Mavis laughed, "What you see, is what you get."

That upset a nervous Charlie. He didn't know how to take it. Thoughts raced through his mind. He decided it was a common phrase and he shouldn't read anything into it. Mavis led him to the sofa in the living room and asked him to sit down. She couldn't help but think it was the same sofa on which Flint had been giving it to her the night before. "I'll get us some coffee, or would you prefer tea." Charlie opted for tea.

Mavis returned with the tea and some plain cookies. The less sugar for Chloe the better. She sat in the big chair which was near enough to set her cup of tea on the coffee table and still get a few of the cookies. Charlie said, "I don't know where to begin."

Mavis was a take charge kind of person. "I'll make it easier for you Charlie. We are attracted to each other, aren't we?" Charlie nodded with enthusiasm. "Why don't we just set our cards on the table. You tell me something about yourself and I'll tell you what little there is about me."

Charlie said he had grown up in nearby West Union, went to high school there, worked in the restaurant and helped in the gas station auto repair shop. Saved enough money to go to college, worked while in college, got a degree, applied for the police academy, was accepted, and here I am."

"Any girl friends you want to tell me about."

"There was a girl in college. We were intimate for a while. She wouldn't wait for me to graduate but wanted to get married while I still had a year to go. I never had any intentions of marrying her and I told her that at the beginning, but she probably thought she could coax me into it. I found out later she had been very promiscuous."

Mavis said there wasn't much for her to tell. Her parents died when she was twelve years old and she was raised by an aunt and her brother Fred. "I graduated from high school where I was active in gymnastics and even won a trophy for tumbling. Billie was nineteen and I was going on twenty. He was still in high school, ready to graduate, and the senior prom was coming up. I agreed to go with Billy and Fred bought me a nice pink gown for the occasion."

"After the prom Billy drove out to the countryside, up on Baldy Mountain and we proceeded to make out. He assured me every girl put out on the night of the prom. So I put out. A month later I missed my period and a month after that I missed my second period. The rest is history. I didn't want to marry him even though he insisted. He was very negligent in that affair and I was naive. I

53

believed a girl couldn't get pregnant the first time she had sex. Boy, was I wrong."

Mavis looked at Charlie with a serious intensity. "But I am so happy to have Chloe, I wouldn't wish it any other way. I have a job offer with the gas company where Fred worked and will take it as soon as Chloe is potty trained and willing to let me get away. Billy's mother Mildred just loves Chloe and would like me to let her raise Chloe, but Chloe is my extra self and I will never part with her. I will share her with Mildred who is her only grandmother, but I will never, never part with her."

Charlie took a cookie and a swig of his tea. "Are there any guys in your life that I should know about. There are no women in my life."

"There's one fellow I see off and on. It's nothing serious, just some one to pass the time and discuss the meaning of life, which until Chloe came along, had no meaning for me."

Charlie was pleased with what he heard. He was about to make some comment when Chloe came staggering into the room, rubbing her sleepy eyes. She went over to Charlie and looked at him, then went to her mother. Mavis hoped Chloe wouldn't say "Fint."

Mavis rose and took her by the hand. "I'll have to change her and get her something to eat. If you and I are going to be an item, you better get used to this."

"I anticipated this situation and I assure you I will enjoy it as much as you do, except for the diapers, of course. " He laughed a melodious chuckle that Mavis was happy to hear. Then he added, "Maybe, you can teach me the art of changing diapers."

Once Chloe was changed they went to the kitchen. Charlie put Chloe in her high chair and clicked the strap between her legs in place. He was about to hand Chloe a cookie when Mavis said "not until she eats other stuff."

Charlie said that if Mildred was happy to baby-sit Chloe, why not have her do so and we will go to a dance in Fairmont on Saturday night. "There's a dance hall where the college students hang out. The band starts at nine o'clock. We will fit right in."

"That's pretty sudden Charlie. Maybe we should think on it a while."

Charlie beamed. "I have been thinking on it a constantly."

"So have I Charlie. After we get settled here, let's the three of us go over to Mildred's and I'll introduce you. She's family, you know."

8. The Coyote Caper

Flint received a call from his partner Ward Hollister concerning their sheep. He said that a coyote had been lurking around the neighborhood. Several people heard it yelping. He had spent several nights on a stake out protecting the four new lambs in the small field. The fence with its six inch wire squares should keep out a coyote, but if the coyote was desperate it could burrow under the fence. He wondered if Flint would take over a couple of evenings and see what he could do. Flint offered to set up his recording equipment and try to call the coyote in to an area where he could get a shot at it. Ward didn't have the sophisticated equipment of most hunters.

A few years ago, Ward Hollister wanted to go into the sheep business and needed financial backing and a partner. He had the land, but not the cash to get started. Flint agreed to put in half of the fifty thousand dollars needed to get the two registered Icelandic Sheep brought in from Canada. Within three years they had a herd of six sheep, a ram and five ewes. An Islandic Sheep ewe can have multiple births, a rarity in most sheep. All registered sheep were tattooed according to the rules of the Canadian Livestock Records Corporation. When a lamb was born without the promise of good growth it was usually sold to a restaurant in Parkersburg.

Ward would do the work and Flint would be a silent partner and receive thirty percent of the profit. However, Flint enjoyed the sheep so much he often went over to the fields and pens and helped Ward out. People with gardens usually came around and took the manure. When the pens needed cleaning Ward would call one of them and they would gladly do the job.

Ward and Flint would also buy a calf in the spring of the year and let it graze all summer. In late autumn they had it butchered and shared the meat with Ward taking most of it. This was just another interesting way of passing the time in the hills.

There wasn't much to do until the ewes were giving birth and the necessary tattoos and registration papers were filed in Canada. Within two years Flint had recouped his investment. Any money he received now would be all profit and reported to the Internal Revenue Service as such. He didn't like the idea of paying taxes on money he had risked.

Flint drove the two miles over to the ranch, as he called it, just before sunset. He unloaded a battery operated tape playing device and set it up on the hillside overlooking the pen that held the ewes and the lambs. He was surprised at the color variations of the four lambs. He thought about genetic variation and how these pure bred sheep should not vary so much in color.

Marian Hollister invited Flint in for a cup of coffee and did he also want a sandwich? "No, coffee would be fine. Where's Ward?"

"Oh, he already went to bed. He has been putting in many odd hours on his job with the stone works and with protecting the sheep at night, he needs the rest. He also has some trouble up north with his brothers and he has to get all of that settled."

"Well, if I can get the coyote, he won't have that to worry

56

about. I just got a new Nikon Buckmasters scope, so I'm anxious to try it out." Pause. " Does he need help with the sheep? I could give him a hand most of next week."

"No, between the two of us, we can handle it. If we need you, I'll give you a ring."

Flint looked at the rosy cheeked, blue eyed Marian. He loved those naturally red puffy lips. But, she was the wife of a friend. Well, Marian was also his friend. He thought of a wise-ass remark, but decided Marian might not see the humor in it, so he said, "I enjoy being around the sheep and wouldn't mind being more involved with them. Our original financial agreement need not be altered on that account."

Miriam said she would discuss it with Ward and if they needed anything other than transportation and feed for the sheep Ward would get back to him.

"Still seeing that woman in Grafton, Flint? Not that it's any of my business."

"Yeah, I see her on weekends. Her name is Michelle. Her son is in the military so we have the house to ourselves. Like me, her spouse flew the coop."

"Us gossipers wondered why you never remarried. We also wondered why Marjorie would walk away from a great looking guy like you with a good solid work ethic. Oh yeah, and no moonshine breath."

"Marjorie kept mumbling about how life was short and she didn't want to waste it in the hills of West Virginia. I don't fault her for that. I could see her point of view. Apparently, I wasn't good enough to hold her here and she went to Florida. Edna said she got a card from her last year. It was from Peru, can you believe that?"

"Everybody who knew Marjorie, liked her. She did have her moments when she appeared to be spaced out. But nobody ever spoke a harsh word about her. Everybody I know liked her."

"Apparently, that included a lot of men."

Miriam decided the theme of that sentence should not be pursued. She reached back to the counter shelf and picked up a postcard. "We had these printed up for the sheep business. What do you think?"

Flint skipped over the address and phone number part and read the text:

The **Icelandic sheep,** (Icelandic: islenska sauokindini) is a breed of domestic sheep. The Icelandic breed is one of the Northern European short-tailed sheep, which exhibit a fluke-shaped, naturally short tail. The Icelandic is a mid-sized breed, generally short legged and stocky, with face and legs free of wool. The fleece of the Icelandic sheep is dual-coated and comes in white as well as a variety of other colors, including a range of browns, grays, and blacks. They exist in both horned and polled strains. Generally left unshorn for the winter, the breed is very cold-hardy. Multiple births are very common in Icelandic ewes. A gene also exists in the breed called the Thoka gene, and ewes carrying it have been known to give birth to triplets, quadruplets, quintuplets, and even sextuplets on occasion.

Ewes can be mated as lambs as early as five to seven months, although many farmers wait until the ewe's second winter before allowing them to breed. They are seasonal breeders and come into estrus around November. There is some variation in this estrus cycle and the breeding season can last up to five months. Descended from the same stock as the Norwegian Spelsau brought to Iceland by the Vikings, Icelandic sheep have been bred for a thousand years in a very harsh environment. Consequently, they are quite efficient herbivores.

Flint put the card on the table. "Very nice." The coffee was almost finished and the sun was setting. Miriam turned on the lights out at the pens. Flint drank the last of his coffee and went out the door, then on to the truck to get his night vision binoculars and his 22 Hornet rifle. On his way up the slope he turned on the playing device. It would play the sound of an injured rabbit at ten minute intervals.

It might be a long fruitless wait and Flint was prepared to do it. He would stay until midnight and then head home. There was no need to use his night vision binoculars since the lights of the pens would be sufficient. The lights were also augmented by a three quarter moon in a cloudless sky.

Sitting with his back against a tree trunk and in view of his recording device and the sheep pens, Flint waited patiently trying not to make any movement. He had been waiting at least an hour and his legs were getting cramped and he stretched them.

The ewes moved in an out of the main pen with the lambs close behind their mothers. Didn't these critturs sleep? The lambs were the size of a Beagle. They seemed to jump for no other reason than joy.

At last there was movement off to the right. Flint put the binoculars up and saw it was a small red fox. It had the characteristic white tip on its tail, so it wasn't a gray. The fox was too little to harm any ewe or week old lambs. The fox was interested in the call of the injured rabbit. Cautiously, it moved in a circular path around the recording device. It moved up to the device and stood confused. It looked around and around, then it moved through the wire mesh and into the sheep compound. As it moved toward one of the small pens that ringed the field, a large ewe came out and charged the fox. It ran to the wire mesh and worked its way through.

Another hour passed and Flint was about to give up when there was again movement off to the right. This time it was the coyote, gray brown, slightly smaller than a German Shepherd which it resembled.

Like the fox before it, the coyote moved in an arc around the recording device. Flint moved the rifle from his lap, put it up to his right cheek and braced the front of it with his left hand on the knee of his bent leg. He looked through the scope and had the head of the coyote in the cross hairs. He pulled the trigger slowly and in a brief second the coyote was writhing on the ground. It squirmed for a few more seconds and then lay motionless.

Flint waited with the rifle ready for another two or three minutes. Then he walked down the hill to the coyote and looked at it. He had hit it in the head as he intended to do. He wanted to keep the pelt in good condition.

The coyote was put on a tarp in the back of the truck. The rifle was put on a gun rack behind the front seat. It was a system that Flint had devised and one that could be locked. Flint attached the lock and went back to get the recording device.

When he was back at the truck Ward was there in his pajamas with Miriam standing beside him. "You got him?" asked Ward. It was a statement as well as an answer.

"Yeah, nice big one. Didn't check the sex. Probably female. I'm going to drop him off at Dan's. He said he would take any fox or coyote I got. He makes hats out of them. He will do anything he can to make an extra buck here in the hills."

"I guess you could say that about all of us," echoed Ward.

9. Saturday - The Date

Mavis was excited as she waited for Charlie to show up. It was a few minutes to the arrival hour of seven o'clock. She had taken Chloe over to Mildred earlier and had spent a lot of time considering what to wear. She didn't have much of a wardrobe so there was not much to debate. She decided on her plaid skirt, white blouse and the plaid vest that matched the skirt. Knee length stockings completed the ensemble. It was October and there was a chill in the air. She

60

unconsciously figured that the skirt would make things easier if she decided to have sex with Charlie, even though she promised herself she would avoid sex on this first date. She was so excited she was willing to pop into bed with Charlie before they went out on the date. Her mind was in a state where thinking normally was not possible.

Charlie arrived at seven on the dot. He must have parked somewhere and waited until the bewitching hour. Mavis asked how the trip from Charleston went. He said he was staying at his mother's in West Union for the weekend and he would drive back to Charleston on Sunday. No problem.

It took a half hour to get to Fairmont and the Appleby Restaurant. Charlie ordered the famous Oriental Salad, small serving. Mavis thought she was too excited and ordered a simple salad and iced tea. They looked at each other. Mavis tried to think of a conversation starter. "You are a long way from home. It must be a four hour drive back to Charleston."

"It will go fast since I will be thinking about you all the way back, just as I thought about you all the way here." Charlie was dressed in black trousers. His top was a plum colored pullover.

The conversation was about his job, Chloe and brother Fred's car that needed some repair. It ran all right, but the sounds it made were unnerving. She never would go further than Clarksburg in it for fear it would break down. She didn't have a cell phone so an emergency would not be pleasant. Charlie wanted to say he would get her a cell phone, but he held back because he didn't want to be purchasing her affection if there was any affection to purchase. They both began to relax and feel that they didn't have to put on a show to impress the other. It seemed to Mavis that she had known Charlie for several years when actually it had been less than a month.

It was eight thirty when they reached the Magic Twanger Tavern where the band performed. They sat in the Toyota and looked at each other without speaking. Charlie became bold and turned Mavis toward him and kissed her on her willing lips. It was a sensational feeling, a first kiss, a ringing in of a new era in each of their lives. They parted and looked deep into each other's eyes. The eyes of Mavis were light green, almost straw colored, Charlie's eyes were very light brown. If the eyes are the windows to the soul, then both souls exhibited sincerity and affection. Mavis broke the spell, "We should go in." Ah, yes, but first, one more kiss.

There was a five dollar per person cover charge and they were informed that they had to spend at least five dollars per person in the establishment. The band did not come cheap. Charlie said that for twenty bucks it would be a cheap night. Mavis didn't know if that was a hint to not order extra drinks or not. Charlie had already spent thirty dollars on dinner. And there was the gasoline. And, "what the hell am I thinking? Can't I enjoy myself without thinking about money?" She would stop thinking about money and she would enjoy herself.

The room was full of young people, college student types, scattered around the room and sitting at tables. Mavis did not look at them but concentrated on Charlie with wonderment in her eyes. He returned her look with his own look of enchantment.

The band began setting up its instruments. There were three members. One apparently was a drummer, another worked a music synthesizer, and the third was setting out a guitar and some brass instruments. They were black musicians.

Charlie ordered a martini, Mavis a glass of white wine. The waitress wanted to know the kind of wine. Mavis said it didn't matter as long as it was white.

Mavis stared at the band and shook her head. Charlie was aware of her puzzled expression. "What's up Mavis?"

"You know what Charlie, I think this is the first time I have ever seen Negroes in the flesh. I see them on TV all the time, but I don't think I ever saw one live and in person." She looked around the room and saw several other blacks among the patrons.

"You got to be kidding. Don't refer to them as colored, Afro-American, or Negroes. Okay." Mavis nodded. "I know, blacks." Charlie said it wasn't a good idea to think in terms of color anyway. We are all God's children."

Mavis assured him that the color didn't bother her, but it was the realization she had been up in the hills all her life and had never seen a black person. Maybe she did when she was a child but didn't remember it. Charlie said it was a good thing Mavis met him, now he was set to show her the world. Unfortunately his world only consisted of the state of West Virginia. Mavis looked around the room and noticed the crowd. Some of the guys were already getting loud and apparently the beer was getting to them.

The band began playing jazz. A few couples began shuffling out to the small dance floor. The band switched from jazz to rock and the dancers acted accordingly. There was a move from jazz to rock, then back to jazz. To Mavis, the dancers were not coordinated to the music, but hey, we are all having a good time. More people went to the dance floor when rock was on and they gyrated and moved with frenetic motion. However, the floor was not crowded with dancers.

It was difficult to talk under the loud music, but some conversation was able to creep through the pounding air waves. Charlie and Mavis went out to the floor and twisted to the rollicking rock music. When they were returning to their seats Mavis said, "I would prefer a slow dreamy dance where you could hold me close." Charlie said that was his idea of dancing also and maybe they should find a place where they played slow dreamy dance music. But, not on short notice. On impulse, Mavis kissed Charlie on the cheek.

The evening was going well. The band broke for intermission. People were able to talk to each other. Mavis had another glass of wine, Charlie switched to beer.

The lead singer of the three piece band walked over to where

Charlie and Mavis were seated. He looked at them, "My old buddy, Officer Charlie Fitch. I thought that was you on the dance floor a while ago. I changed my mind when I saw this gorgeous woman. No gorgeous woman would be seen with you. But, here you are."

"Hello, Lennie. I didn't recognize you with your shades, besides this is my first date with Mavis and she has all my attention. So, don't mess it up by telling stories about me." It was obvious to Mavis that they were on friendly terms.

Lennie was a tall. thin black man, with a hazelnut complexion. His hair was straight and combed back. His eyes were set back in his head and were separated by a thin pointed nose. Thin lips and a wide mouth completed his features. Also, flashing white teeth.

"You working undercover Charlie?"

"No Lennie, I'm off duty. Have a seat and I'll buy you a drink." Lennie sat next to Mavis and ordered a jigger of rum. Mavis stared at him and surveyed his lean body.

Lennie turned to Mavis. "I am Leonard Gibbs. Charlie busted me once and it cost me ten Gs. However, we are friends and he was just doing his job." He looked at Charlie. "There will be a lot of weed going around tonight, I hope you don't disturb the atmosphere. It's part of my budget."

"No Lennie, I think it should be legalized and I don't pursue my official duties in that direction."

Lennie felt the look of Mavis on him. He didn't know how to interpret it. "Why you lookin at me like that Mavis?"

"Sorry Leonard, you just fascinate me, I guess. Here we are sitting with a great musician. Besides being almost drunk, I'm awe struck."

Leonard turned to Charlie. "She's putting me on, right."

"To some extent Lennie. Do you know that you are the first black person Mavis has ever seen in her life, up close."

"Is that a fact?" He flashed a toothy smile at Mavis who said that she lived in the hills all her life, never got to the city, and there were no African Americans in the hills."

"We are Americans, and we don't like being labeled differently than any other Americans."

Mavis apologized and Leonard said he understood and was just making a prepared statement and thought it had some humor. He asked if Mavis would like to touch his skin. She reached out and placed her hand on his bare forearm and moved it slowly up to his muscle. "Very nice and cool." She felt she must be getting drunk. She squeezed the muscle.

Leonard flashed white teeth. "Would you like to feel other parts of my body?"

Mavis withdrew her hand. "No, not at this time."

Charlie laughed. "You saying, maybe at some other time."

"No, that was just a routine response." She turned to Lennie. "I just met you Lennie, and I do like you already. Maybe we'll meet again."

Charlie said, "I hope not." Laughed.

Leonard reached into a pocket on his shirt and pulled out a card and handed it to Mavis. "Here's my card for you to remember me by. And I like you too Mavis and hope we do meet again. How do you like my music?"

"It's okay, but I was hoping for some slow dreamy dance music where I could cuddle up to Charlie. This is our first date and I want to make a good impression."

Leonard flashed his white teeth again. "I'm a virtuoso. I can sing and play any type of music ever invented. Even opera. What slow dreamy thing can you think of and I'll play it for you tonight."

Mavis thought on it. "How about Unchained Melody? Do you know it? Or is that too old fashioned."

"No, I can arrange it to slow dance and give you a one and a two beat."

"What's a one and a two beat."

"Well when people dance slow dances, they usually take one step, pause, and then take two steps. You know, kinda get your feet moving in time with the beat. You'll see. But, first we got to do some loud stuff and get the hop heads rattled. Gotta get back, Bubba is looking for me."

Leonard rose and shook hands with Charlie. "Good to see you buddy." Turned and offered his hand to Mavis who clasped it with both of hers. "Thanks for coming over Leonard."

The band rocked the house until the rafters shook. A few couples moved their bodies in fantastic leaps, turns and bounds. They seemed to be professional performers. Black and black, white and white, and black and white.

After processing six pieces, Lennie went to the microphone. "We will play a slow dance number requested by a new found friend of mine. I hope you will bear with me on this."

The synthesizer began playing intro music as Lennie stepped up to the mike. Mavis took Charlie by the hand and led him to the empty dance floor.

A silver voice sang out, "Lonely river flows to the sea, to the sea, open arms of the sea."

Mavis put her head against Charlie chin. They moved slowly. "Lonely river says, wait for me, wait for me, I'll be coming home, wait for me."

Couples rushed to the floor and soon the small area was crowded and our couple found it difficult to navigate. Mavis and Charlie swayed in place. Leonard mumbled, "well I'll be damned" then continued singing " Oh my love, my darling, I hunger for your touch, a long lonely time."

Charlie kissed Mavis on the cheek. Other couples were also kissing. "I'll be coming home, wait for me." Mavis kissed Charlie on the mouth. They stopped dancing for a moment and held the kiss and the embrace that went with it.

The dance ended and the crowd applauded with enthusiasm and didn't move off the floor. Leonard looked at Bubba who hunched his shoulders and nodded. They began to play rock and everyone left the floor. Some new couples came out to twist to the rhythm.

It was obvious that the slow dance had caught on and the band responded with several more dreamy dance tunes. They ended the evening with the clear silver voice of Lennie singing Unchained Melody to a crowded dance floor. They would use the song as the theme to end every evening they played in the future.

Back in the car Charlie and Mavis kissed passionately. "Not on the first date," said Mavis. "Why not," asked Charlie, "you know as well as I do that we go together. We are both ready."

"I don't want you to be disappointed and not ever see you again."

"I promise that won't happen. I feel so attached to you I know that will never happen."

Mavis stopped kissing and asked if Charlie had brought a condom. Charlie said he thought Mavis would be on the pill. Aren't all girls on the pill these days? Mavis said she was on the pill but she would like Charlie to use a condom, at least for a few times and until she and he were more accountable, whatever that meant. Charlie said he would go back in the Magic Twanger and get a pack of condoms. He cursed himself for not being better prepared.

He was able to get the condoms from a vending machine in the men's room. When it was over and they were driving home, Mavis said that Charlie could start staying over at her place on Saturday nights, but not tonight.

They would get in one more session on the sofa before Charlie would go to stay over at his mother's. Charlie said there was still one more condom left over from the pack. Mavis said it would be a shame to throw it away.

10. Sunday Maneuvers

Flint picked up Jimmy Critchlow on his way to the rendezvous point with Captain Earl Hazzard and the others. Jimmy expressed the opinion that they shouldn't be practicing aggressive offensive maneuvers but should be concentrating on perimeters and such action to protect their settlements from intruders. They had often discussed the mob moving west along Route 50 once the stuff hit the fan.

Flint thought Earl was preparing to take the fight to the enemy, whoever that was. Jimmy couldn't think of a prospective enemy either, except maybe to hold off the government agents, like at Ruby Ridge and Waco. Even that would be a defensive maneuver. Flint said they should go along with Earl until the time was appropriate to challenge him and his supposed authority and head the militia group in another direction. He thought Earl was responsible for the disaster that was Fred Kramer. Jimmy agreed and added, "It's a fine October Day, let's have a lot of fun."

Jimmy asked Flint about his wife Marjorie. Edna told Jimmy's wife Sophie that she saw Marjorie in Clarksburg with some well dressed rich looking guy. Flint was aware of that, since Edna had called him. Edna said Marjorie had dyed her hair an orange red and really looked tough. She was supposed to still be in Florida. "I thought maybe she made a mistake," offered Flint, " but I don't think Edna makes many mistakes. I trust her most outlandish gossip to be accurate."

"You were seen leaving the home of Mavis Kramer early one morning. Of course that was all over the hills the next day."

Flint admitted to being at the Kramer house, but said that he had fallen asleep after drinking two bottles of home made wine and Mavis didn't want to wake him and to hell with the neighbors. Jimmy's opinion was that any man would be a fool to turn down a chance of sex with Mavis. Flint admitted he was no fool and if the opportunity ever arose he would be ready for it. At this point he had nothing but sympathy for Mavis and what now must be a tricky financial situation. He added that Mavis and the cop Charlie Fitch had a thing going at this time. Jimmy said, "Really. I liked that guy right off. Felt as if he was a younger brother of mine."

Flint wondered why Jimmy and Sophie didn't have children. He said that Marjorie couldn't have children and that was what may have caused what he thought were mental problems. Jimmy said that he and Sophie would start having children when she turned thirty five next year. They didn't want to spend their youth raising kids, but

69

would really like them when they were a little older and more stable mentally. Sophie's parents ran an antique buying and selling business in Ohio, "you know, old pottery, spoons, coins, that sort of thing. They already have two grandchildren from her brother, but they would give the world for Sophie to have children. Well, starting next year, they can begin giving her some of that world. We really don't need anything from them, but we will accept whatever they offer to make them feel they are contributing to our family welfare."

It was almost two o'clock as Flint and Jimmy pulled along the side of the road and waited for the other maneuver participants to appear. They were the first to arrive. Soon two pick-up trucks came on the scene. One pulled up behind them and the other moved in front. These were followed by the SUV of Earl Hazzard who had three other people with him. The people in the Hazzard vehicle unloaded quickly. One of them was Ray Pflipps, dressed in an ill fitting camouflage outfit.

Flint looked at Jimmy. "What the hell. I thought Pflipps had gone back to Tennessee.

Jimmy laughed. "Don't you know anything Flint. He has been sexing Alicia Atkins ever since he got here. Sophie thinks with Elmer's approval. Elmer goes to work, the kids go to school and that leaves Alicia and Ray home alone. There's no honor among thieves."

"What evidence do you have?" Flint had humor in his voice, "for that unfounded accusation."

"Our house is uphill from Elmer's and we can see right into their kitchen and living room. We can get a close-up with our binoculars. Sophie saw Pflipps putting it to Alicia on their sofa sometime around noon almost every day since he's been here."

Flint laughed. "It doesn't pay to have neighbors. How do you know that it is with Elmer's approval?"

"Well, Flint, if my wife Sophie had a chance to screw some famous person I wouldn't stand in the way. It's an experience that comes once in a lifetime. Say, some movie star or national personality. She wouldn't stand in my way either."

"Maybe, you have a point there, but I don't consider Ray Pflipps would be desirable at any level. I always thought Alicia had an attractive body, built for comfort, not speed. Can't see why she would want to waste it on the likes of Ray Pflipps."

"Well, anyway, Sophie spends a lot of time with the binoculars and enjoying the sex scene."

Earl Hazzard was assembling the group. Flint grinned. "How am I going to get serious today with that knowledge. Does anybody else know?"

"I only told you. I don't think Sophie has spread any of this around yet. So don't you go gossiping. I doubt if Sophie would ever tell anyone about it. I don't know why I told you. Maybe some secrets are too heavy for one person to carry alone,"

They went over to the group that had gathered around Earl Hazzard and Ray Pflipps. Everyone had a rifle. Earl counted the men. There were no women. Flint noticed Elmer Atkins standing with Ray Pflipps. Earl spoke. "There are fourteen of us. We will divide into two groups. I will head one group and Lieutenant Flint Haloway will head the other." He turned to Flint. "Pick out your six."

Flint didn't have to pick. Six men quickly moved to where Flint was standing. One of them was Jimmy Critchlow. Flint moved further to one side, his men followed. The other men moved nearer to Earl Hazzard and Ray Pflipps.

Earl walked over the few feet and handed Flint a whistle. He had a whistle strapped to his neck, took it in his hand and blew a single long note. "Notice this is not a referee whistle. It is a ship's whistle. Flint and I will make up signals for our own group. We will try to use hand and other visual signals instead of making noise. I have printed orders for each squad." He handed Flint a half sheet of computer paper. Flint took a quick look at it. Earl held his sheet in front of him.

Earl interrupted his delivery to say that Ray Pflipps has decided to stay over and give us another inspiration talk. This one will feature Waco. Spread the word.

The procedure for this maneuver was further explained by Earl. " Each squad will walk about a mile down the road in different directions. Flint's group will go that way and my group this a way."

Earl had the sheet in front of him. "At 14:30 hours, both squads would start up the mountain toward the top. They will proceed about two hundred yards, about the length of two football fields and wait until 15:00. At 15:10 we will move up the mountain another two hundred yards. At that point we will encounter a wall of rock. There are passages through the rocks and you will have to find them."

Ray Pflipps was not one to let other people do the talking. He butted in. "Keep in line going up the hill. Keep about a hundred feet between you and keep sight of the man on each side of you."

"Good advice Ray." Earl did appreciate the input which gave him the feeling he was on a par with Ray Pflipps.

Floyd Maynard looked at Ray Pflipps. "Hey, Ray, I just heard your broadcast on the radio. How did you do that?"

Ray laughed. "I have about a hundred broadcasts ready to go and when I'm away, my sound manager takes over and dubs things in when necessary." Most everyone smiled and Pflipps felt he was at home with a segment of his flock of listeners.

Earl continued. "You will get set at the new location and wait until 16:00. Then move the rest of the way until you are in the woods just below the abandoned two story house that's in the clearing. At that point I will send a runner to Flint and he will send a runner to me to verify that we are all in place. Remember the hallmark of the army is to sit and wait, so be patient. Stay there, communicate only by hand signals and wait until 17:15. At that time, on the signal from your squad leader, commence firing into the building. Fire only two shots and wait for orders from the squad leader. There are still some window panes in the place and you might want to zero in on those in order to gauge the accuracy of your shots. Part of the roof is caved in, but there are some gutters still on the building. You might want to take a crack at them. One of my boys and I went up here yesterday checking it out and we climbed the mountain so there should be no problem with timing. Any questions?"

Flint said that when they arrived at the top of the hill they should form an EL shape with both squads. That way they wouldn't be shooting over each other's heads. Earl said that was good and when his squad got to the top, Flint was to stay in place and his squad would form the other side of the EL shape.

Nobody seemed to have any other question or comment. "Okay, let's go." Flint started up the slight rise in the road and six men followed him. Earl led his group down the road.

Flint had estimated that he had gone a mile. He could walk a mile in twenty minutes so he timed the walk. Not many words were spoken during that twenty minutes. When the approximate position had been reached Flint looked at his group. He wanted Jimmy Critchlow to be near him so he put Jimmy to his right. Alfie and Coach were wearing orange hunting jackets so he put them on the ends of the squad where they would be easily seen. Dan, Billy, and Eddie made up the rest of his group and he spaced them accordingly.

73

They waited in place. Flint looked at his watch. It was 2:30, 14:30 military time. A tweet on the whistle was the signal to start climbing.

The slope from the road was not steep and the estimated two hundred yards was reached quickly. Everyone was in place and sitting. Flint waited until 3:00 then gave a tweet on the whistle. Everyone in the squad moved upward. They came to the stone cliff that Earl had predicted. Each man got above it the best he could. Flint could see Eddie with his rifle strapped on his back climbing almost hand over hand hanging on to extended roots. Flint found a narrow passage up through the rock face and motioned for Jimmy to come over. When they got above the rocks Jimmy went back to his assigned position and looked for Dan who was between him and Coach. He waved to Alfie who waved back.

It was up through mountain laurel and small birch and maple trees, over rocks and bare roots. Flint kept checking the men to his sides. He waved to Eddie and waited. Eddie waved back with both arms which was the signal that the other men were keeping up with the ascent.

At 4:00 they arrived at the point where they could see the dilapidated two story building standing like some ancient buffalo on its knees waiting to die. Many of the gray old boards of the siding were hanging down at odd angles. There were four windows on this side of the house and the two upper windows still had glass in some of the panes. Half the roof had caved in and the half that was still intact had shingles on it. Flint wondered about the many happy times that must have occurred here and then he thought the name Camp Mistake might indicate that some of the times were not happy.

There was a hand pump over a well in the front of the house. They were not very smart people if they looked for water on top of the hill instead of at the bottom or at least where some impenetrable rock held an elevated water table. That one item alone deserved the title Camp Mistake. Maybe the well was connected to the rain water draining off the roofs. Anyway, there was a reason for calling it Camp Mistake.

Flint called the group to him. He was on his knees and the others were on their knees in front of him. He spoke in a low voice telling them to spread out, they still had a half hour or more to wait. Dan and Coach unwrapped candy bars. Coach offered one to Alfie who accepted it. Flint said he would give them the signal when they should move to the edge of the clearing. He asked Eddie to move along to the other side of the ridge and go to Earl's group and tell him they were in place. He told Eddie to be sure and remind Earl to form the EL shape so they wouldn't be shooting over each other's heads. Eddie took off and the other members of the squad dispersed to their assigned positions. Flint would tweet the whistle a minute before they should move forward. On the second tweet they should fire their three shots into the building. Coach said, "I thought it was two shots." Flint said, "Fire three anyway."

Elmer Atkins was the runner sent by Earl. His message was that they were all in place except Ray Pflipps had lagged behind, but they could see him coming up the hillside and he would be in place with the rest of them at the appointed hour. Flint told Elmer to move down and get set on the other side of Alfie. "Ask Alfie what the procedure would be to commence firing."

The wait seemed long but at 5:14 (17:14 military time) Flint blew his whistle. The squad moved forward and at 5:15 Flint blew his whistle again and a volley of shots slammed into the building from different sides of the ridge. The firing ceased and the squad waited for orders to start firing again.

"Stop, you bastards." A voice was crying out from the building. "Help, Stop."

Flint yelled. "Cease firing," and raced to the building. Before he got there a young man came out the door-less entrance. He looked at Flint. "What the hell is going on. Good thing I was kneeling on the

75

floor or I might have been killed." Earl arrived.

"Anybody with you?" asked Earl.

"No, I am backpacking the old Duckworth Trail that runs through here and decided to stop off in this abandoned building for the evening. I was on my knees getting my bed roll in order in the dry part when the bullets came through the walls, I hit the floor and flattened out."

Flint thought it was a good thing that most of the shooters were probably aiming at the upper windows and the hanging gutters. He looked at the side of the building and saw that not everyone was aiming at the upper story. Many bullet holes could be seen at different heights on the side of the building.

11. Second Coming of Ray Pflipps

It was Tuesday evening and the second event featuring Ray Pflipps was about to begin. Word about the meeting must have spread quickly. The small meeting hall of the Mountaineer Militia was jammed. What else could the hill people do for entertainment and socialization? People were directed outside to the windows that would be opened so they could hear the presentation. There were over a dozen women in the group and they were given seats inside the building by the gentlemen of the hills. Flint figured that the word about Alicia Atkins and Ray Pflipps got around and the women would be watching those two performers rather than listening to the presentation.

Earl Hazzard called the meeting to order and said there would be another training session that would be discussed at the next regular meeting which was two weeks away. He hoped the people listening by the windows and open door would not be uncomfortable and invited the men who were not members of the militia to come to the meeting in November and they "could see what we are about."

Earl didn't prolong the introduction. It was getting cold inside despite the heat generated by over seventy bodies. "Radio personality, Ray Pflipps, ladies and gentlemen." This initiated a good applause."

Ray Pflipps paused dramatically. The audience was hushed. "Again, I would like to thank your group Earl for inviting me." Flint thought to himself that the militia group had nothing to do with it and it was Earl's idea. Pflipps continued. "And again I would like to thank Alicia and Elmer Atkins for their outstanding hospitality." Everyone turned to look at Alicia at one end of the back row of seats, but not at Elmer who was seated at the other end of the same back row.

Waco According to Ray Pflipps

The lawyer for one of the survivors said at one of the U.S. government 'investigations', or rather, whitewashes: In this country when people are accused of a crime they are arrested and given a trial — that's due process. If found guilty of murder then maybe they are killed. We don't just kill them first — which is what happened at Waco.

Many people believe that David Koresh, or the Branch Davidians, were responsible for the deaths of the 74 men, women and children who died in the inferno at Waco on April 19, 1993. This is the story that the FBI put out. It is a lie. The guns they had in the compound were legal. The local sheriff investigated and found no basis for complaints against them. These were law-abiding American citizens, even if they thought differently than most other folks. They trusted the U.S. Constitution to ensure their political rights, but they were murdered by agents acting under the authority of the U.S. government.

Waco occurred under the presidency of Bill Clinton, with Janet Reno and Wesley Clark in supporting roles. Already back in 1993 the US government demonstrated its contempt for the

American people by carrying out a massacre in order to "demonstrate" on prime time TV, its supposed "authority." This is a favorite tactic of fascist governments, a tactic favored by oppressive governments. Following the usurpation of the presidency in 2000 by the psychopath George W. Bush and the subsequent installation of he insane John Ashcroft as Bush's thug, things became much worse.

Not many people today realize that when the Bureau of Alcohol, tobacco, and Firearms, the BATF, agents raided the Branch Davidians church and home, they did so with guns blazing. Never mind the children and women in the church. The government deliberately sabotaged negotiations with Koresh and the Davidians to prevent their exit from the compound. Their goal was to destroy the building and the damaging evidence, even if it meant the massacre of dozens of women and children who were all witnesses to the brutal attack. This is not just my opinion. This is what a woman named Carol Moore reported in a book on the subject.

After the initial attack, the FBI and the U.S. Army took over the butchery and initiated a 51 day siege. They put out all night, very loud, broadcasts that deprived the compound residents of much needed sleep.

David Koresh was writing a complex explanation of the meaning of Seven Seals at this time and said they would surrender upon completion of the document. At dawn on April 19, 1993, army tanks rammed holes in the main building and pumped CS gas into the building despite their knowledge that there were more than a dozen children housed there. The main building was saturated with CS gas and spilled kerosene.

Just after noon two U.S. Military pyrotechnic devices were fired into the main building. This ignited a fire which spread rapidly through the complex killing 74 men, women, and children. To add insult to all of this, when the fire died down the BATF flag was hoisted aloft, just like a signal in a battlefield victory. The building was razed to cover up the evidence of this premeditated murder of innocent civilians. Most Americans believed this could never happen in this country.

Elmer Atkins rose from the crowd. Ray Pflipps stopped his tirade and acknowledged him. "Would you give us the chronological events that transpired during this siege."

Pflipps was pleased, "Be glad to." Flint thought that the question was prearranged.

On February 28, about two months before the conflagration, David Koresh was interviewed by CNN from inside the compound. The CIA didn't like the outcome so they told CNN and a Dallas radio station to conduct no further interviews. On this day, a man named Michael Shroeder was shot dead when he tried to get back in the compound after a brief interview with CIA personnel. A call was put out by the CIA for anyone who wishes to leave the compound to do so and that they would be safe. Four children left the compound at this time. Late in the day David Koresh talked to members of the Dallas radio station.

The FBI cut off outside communications completely. This included telephone contact. They didn't have cell phones in those days. Big smile from Pflipps. David Koresh said he would surrender his group if he was allowed to broadcast a message on Dallas radio. The broadcast was made, but Koresh told negotiators that God told him to remain in the building and wait for more messages. At that time 19 more children left the compound. The children were released in pairs two by two, just like the Noah's Ark. Ninety eight people were still in the building.

There were two government groups fighting for control of the siege. One wanted more negotiations and the other wanted to blast the compound to smithereens. Unfortunately, the latter group won out.

Koresh told eleven people to leave the compound. They were immediately taken into custody by the feds and were hastily interviewed. The more sensible negotiators wanted to do something about the children still in the compound. Their efforts were thwarted. All power and water to the compound was discontinued.

During the siege a number of scholars who study religious groups attempted to persuade the FBI that the siege tactics being

79

used by government agents would only create the impression within the Davidians that they were part of a Biblical "end-of-times" confrontation that had cosmic significance. This would likely increase the chances of a violent and deadly outcome. The religious scholars pointed out that while on the outside, the beliefs of the group may have appeared to be extreme, to the Davidians, their religious beliefs were deeply meaningful, and they were willing to die for them. This is recorded in a number of books on the subject.

At around noon on the final fateful day, three fires broke out almost simultaneously in different parts of the building. The government maintains the fires were deliberately started by Davidians. Survivors maintain the fires were accidentally or deliberately started by the assault. As the fire spread, Davidians were prevented from escaping; others refused to leave and eventually became trapped. In all, only nine people left the building during the fire. The remaining Davidians, including the children, were either buried alive by rubble, suffocated by the effects of the fire or shot. Many who suffocated from the fire were killed by smoke or carbon monoxide inhalation and other causes as fire engulfed the building. Footage of the incident was being broadcast worldwide via television.

In all, 76 died and nine survived the fire on April 19. Despite significant primary source video, much dispute remains as to the actual events of the siege.

When we analyze the situation from a logical and ethical standpoint the conclusion is straightforward, the Davidians were murdered by the U. S. Government, simply for being different. There was a smattering of applause. Ray Pflipps was ready for questions and comments. Several men stood up. Ray apparently recognized Jimmy Critchlow from the maneuvers and pointed to him.

Jimmy had a small sheet of paper in his hand. "We certainly appreciate you're being here colonel. I did some computer research on the topic when I heard you were going to stay over. Here are some interesting facts." Jimmy began to read. "During the siege, the FBI sent a video camera to the Davidians. In the video tape made by

Koresh's followers, Koresh introduced his children and his "wives" to the FBI negotiators including several minors who claimed to have had babies fathered by Koresh. The statement claims Koresh had fathered perhaps 14 of the children who stayed with him in the compound." Jimmy looked up. "What do you think of that aspect of the situation?"

Ray Pflipps smiled. "Well, we all like good sex." Flint looked at Alicia who had a pious expression on her face.

"The fact of the Davidians and their sexual habits is immaterial to the central point of this discussion. Everyone should be entitled to his own sexual and religious beliefs. The fact is that the government acted hastily and with proper negotiation could have spared the lives of all those people. If David Koresh had violated some law then he should have been tried in a proper court and not tried in a military assault." This statement was followed by a smattering of applause.

Eddie rose and was recognized by Ray Pflipps. "I read where a woman with a computer disc surrendered before the fire started and the disc contained the manuscript of David Koresh. Do you know what happened to it."

"You are referring to Ruth Riddle and the manuscript was the interpretation and meaning of the Seven Seals. I don't know what happened to it. Probably confiscated by the FBI."

Eddie sat down and Dan stood up. He was recognized. "The write-ups I read said the compound children had been physically and sexually abused long before the standoff. Got anything on that?"

Pflipps huffed. "That was probably the justification used by President Clinton and Attorney General Janet Reno. The allegations of sexual abuse were never substantiated. Government statements have alluded to those allegations, but I emphasize they were never proven. In fact, survivors say those events never occurred, at least they never witnessed such events."

81

Ray, of course, had the last word and that last word was "the government is often the abuser of the people rather than the protector of the people."

12. Wednesday Night, Mavis and a Big Surprise

It was Wednesday and Flint was curious as to how the date with Charlie turned out for Mavis. They would discuss it later, since they both were anxious to get in the sexual aspect of their relationship before any serious discussion would ensue.

The sexual aspect was fantastic as both partners seemed to put in an extra effort along with much kissing and hugging. Flint was not required to use a condom. Mavis did not think of Charlie at any time during the encounter. She had a sense of freedom and security about her. Flint was there and he was a great example of the masculine species.

Flint dressed. He had left his shoes in the living room. Mavis slid into her blouse and skirt. She was wearing knee length stockings and hadn't taken them off for the event.

They left the bedroom and settled on the sofa of the living room. Flint had brought a bottle of wine. "I figure we should only share one bottle. We don't want to make this into a drunken event. This wine came from Australia, would you believe it? Michelle said Australia produced world class wine. I got it in Grafton. Imagine, Australian wine showing up in Grafton." He poured them each a half glass.

"I'm not a wine expert, but this is really good." Mavis took another sip and rolled it around on her tongue, swallowed it and put her tongue against Flint's clean shaven cheek. Then she ran her tongue over his lips.

"Are you trying to turn me on again?"

"No, I just want to let you know that despite my weekend, I still love you and find you desirable."

Of course this statement led to a discussion of the week end from both directions. Mavis admitted having sex with Charlie, but insisting he use a condom. Flint asked why the restriction. She said she wasn't sure about Charlie not having any sexual transmitted diseases and she didn't like the idea of him shooting sperm laden fluids directly into her. She didn't mind Flint doing that and she was home with Flint where she could douche it out if it made her uncomfortable.

That seemed a reasonable explanation, but maybe a little curious. Flint asked her how was it with Charlie? She said, "very enjoyable, but he isn't quite in your league. I hope to change that in the future. How are things in Grafton."

"Kinda upsetting. I told you about Michelle's son being in the U.S. Marines and working in the embassy in Iraq. Well, there was a raid on the embassy and Lawrence was shot in the stomach and kneecap. Maybe somewhere else. It will be months of recovery. Once he gets stabilized, Michelle was informed he could come home to recuperate. He's the same age as you. Michelle had him when she was eighteen."

"I guess the son will be home in a few days. There goes your Saturday nights." She took another swig of wine.

"No, not really. Larry and I are good friends and he appreciates my relationship with his mother. His father abandoned them when Larry was around three and his mother got the job with the county, so they didn't hurt for money. It wasn't easy, but now Michelle has a comfortable life and Larry is all she lives for."

"I think she lives for you Flint. Any woman would be happy to be tied up with you on a permanent basis. You're handsome, intelligent and gainfully employed. You don't have a reckless lifestyle and you are not one to boast or brag or try to show how tough you are."

That was some endorsement. Flint didn't know what to say. He wanted to tell Mavis that she was beautiful, intelligent, resourceful, and a good mother to Chloe. He didn't say those things because he felt that a reciprocal compliment would seem like it was extracted.

"There is a rumor going around." Mavis looked serious. "Someone claims to have seen your wife Marjorie in Clarksburg. I thought she was in Florida."

"So did I. It was Edna who claims to have seen her. Said she had hair dyed orange or some color like that. I should have divorced her on grounds of desertion when she took off for Florida with Lord knows who. Someone said she went down with a guy named Jasper. We were never meant for each other. We knew it from the start. I was happy when she took off. Heard this guy Jasper had a job with a fishing fleet. Coach said this Jasper was an okay guy. He never had any trouble with him. Should have sent him a thank you note." He laughed and Mavis laughed with him. But, deep down inside Flint was hurt by the incident and he often wondered why he never discussed with Marjorie what was bothering her.

Flint rose and went to the kitchen window. "Looks like it's starting to snow. Well, it is November and we should be getting some snow about now. That will make tracking the deer a lot easier."

"Do you still hunt?"

"Not anymore." Flint said he stopped hunting a while ago. He didn't know what to do with the venison he harvested. For years he contributed the meat to the food bank in Clarksburg, but now he simply delighted in the stories of other hunters. He hunted rabbits and squirrels and enjoyed cooking them in various ways. He had a months supply of squirrel meat in his freezer. Would Mavis like some of it? She would. He would bring her over a couple of pounds in a day or two and some hints on preparation. He said he would also bring over some frozen hamburger patties from the last steer he and Ward Hollister had raised. She reminded him that her brother Fred was a good hunter and she was very adept at cooking wild game.

Flint went back to the living room. Instead of sitting on the sofa he sat in the big stuffed adjustable chair and put his stocking feet on the coffee table. Instead of going to the sofa Mavis sat on his

84

lap and put her head on his chest. "You know Flint, I could easily live with you and be happy."

"That would work out. But, why waste your life? You still have some living to do."

Mavis was on a sexual roll. She couldn't seem to get sex off her mind. She now had two great guys at her disposal and she wanted to take advantage of that situation.

"So do you Flint. We will take it slowly. I sure do like you." She began kissing him on the neck, ears, and cheeks. He felt her breasts, pulled apart her unbuttoned blouse and kissed them."

"Things are going so good Mavis, I hate to leave you tonight."

"No, you have to get to work tomorrow and I have a busy day. I'll be going to interview the admissions woman at Clarksburg University and the budget officer. Charlie said the government will give me a scholarship and I thought if things can be worked out I'll become an elementary teacher and have Chloe in my class."

That would be great. Flint wondered why she hadn't mentioned it before, since it was a momentous undertaking. It had been rattling around in the brain of Mavis for some time, but her discussion with Charlie clinched it and she made the call to Clarksburg. Yes, there were public funds available. Mildred would be more than happy to take care of her granddaughter.

Flint gave her an extra big kiss before he went out the kitchen door. It was one thirty and a bright moon reflected off the newly fallen snow. He thought about Marjorie and Florida and mused that they never had snow in Florida and it was beautiful. He certainly would miss the seasons if he went away. October had been a perfect month in West Virginia. It was now November and not far behind October as a great month in Flint's mind.

Flint and Mavis both lived in the settlement of Buckeye so there was no need to drive to her place. He walked jauntily along, whistling softly under his breath and took in the cold exhilarating air. He wondered if the neighbors were still up and if some busybody was registering the time he had left Mavis.

There was a light on in his house as Flint approached it. He didn't remember leaving the light on in the kitchen. He twisted the knob on the kitchen door cautiously, then threw it open and stood on the porch as the light from the kitchen engulfed him. There sitting at the kitchen table having a cup of something was the expatriate Marjorie. Flint strode in.'

"What the hell are you doing here?"

"I live here, remember?"

"The hell you do. You moved away five years ago and you have no rights in this house."

Marjorie smiled. "I don't think you remember George, the house is in both our names. So I am half owner and am here claiming my rights. I waited up for you, since I assume you wouldn't want to be in bed with me. It would be a good way to welcome me home. Just tell me where I can sleep. I am tired, extremely tired, and need to sleep. We can discuss this in the morning."

Flint quickly surveyed his spouse. She had the orange red hair so aptly described by Edna. Marjorie was dressed in a beige dress with a floral design. A white belt was around her waist. Her face was haggard for a thirty five year old, puffy, eyes with bags under them, and a skin that looked like the white topping of a week old cupcake. She crossed her legs and exposed some nice thighs. There was a small scar on the left side of her chin that wasn't there when she took off more than five years ago.

Flint was now calm. "You took me by surprise. I'll have to sort this out. You can sleep in the small bedroom upstairs. There are sheets and blankets in the closet. The sink and the toilet in the bathroom work. The other bedroom upstairs is not ready for guests. I have a big day of work scheduled for tomorrow. We can discuss a settlement on the house and other things tomorrow."

Marjorie was not smiling."I will tell you this up front George. I intend to live here until I get back on my feet. Maybe, even sell the house. I'll keep out of your way and expect you to keep out of mine.

We can discuss grocery and other arrangements. I must get to sleep. Goodnight, my prince, and sweet dreams." She picked up the suitcase beside her and headed upstairs. She left her coat hanging over a kitchen chair.

Flint went to the bathroom, brushed his teeth, slid off his trousers and shorts and washed his penis in the sink. Picked up his trousers and shorts and headed for his bedroom. As he lay in bed he could hear Marjorie in the room above him shoving furniture around.

The next day at work he told Eddie and Coach that Marjorie had arrived with a vengeance at his house last night. He went into the details of their late night conversation. He thought about his situation constantly during the day. This was a special day of work and he was able to eat his packed lunch in the lunchroom with Eddie, Coach and a few other guys.

Both friends said they sympathized with Flint and wondered how they might be able to help him out of this situation. Flint said he would have to work it out. He might have to sell the house to settle this matter, and he was still married. He should have initiated a divorce long ago, but he thought he would never get married again, so why bother getting a divorce.

Eddie asked, "How did you feel when you opened the door and saw Marjorie there?"

"My first impulse was to kill her."

Flint immediately realized he should not have said that, since everyone in the small lunch room could follow the conversation. He said, "No, I guess my first impulse was to grab her and throw her and her suitcase out the door."

In the afternoon, Flint's mind went from irrationality to rationality. Perhaps, he and Marjorie could work something out temporarily. He would insist they have no visitors. They would buy their own food and run their own vehicles. However, it appeared that Marjorie had no vehicle since there was none on the road or in the small driveway beside Flint's Chevy Silverado.

87

It was Thursday evening. Marjorie was not in the house. Flint had showered, made supper, and waited for his estranged spouse to appear. Eventually, Marjorie appeared and said she had to go to Clarksburg and asked Alicia Atkins to give her a ride so she could open up a bank account and buy a second hand car. She bought a ten year old Ford. She sat at the table with Flint.

Flint thought Alicia would be more than willing to give Marjorie a ride. There was so much juicy material to be obtained during an hour ride. The material would soon be spread over the three patch settlements like a fresh coat of paint.

Marjorie had recovered from her condition of the previous evening. Her face had lost its puffiness and the whites around her green eyes were no longer streaked with red. The rumpled floral dress had been pressed and the orange hair had been neatly combed. She was acceptable. Actually, Flint found her quite attractive.

Marjorie tried to be pleasant, or at least, civil, but Flint was not in the mood for conciliation. He asked, "Where did you get the money for the car. I assumed you were broke and that's why you returned."

"No, I missed you George, and wanted to have sex with you again." She laughed a shrill that sent chills into Flint.

'I don't think that will ever happen again. You didn't say where you got the money. Did you have a job and save it up? You probably were into something illegal, not prostitution, because you like to give it away."

Marjorie ignored that comment and pulled over her purse. "I didn't put all my money in the bank, just a part of it. And, I do have a lot of money." She opened the purse and took out a stack of bills held together with a rubber band and pushed them toward Flint. "This will help pay for my share of the groceries, utilities, and household expenses."

Flint took the wad of bills and quickly riffled them. There were about thirty bills in the pack, all with a portrait of Ulysses S. Grant. "You got any more of these?"

"Yes I do, many more and I don't want you going through my stuff. My small, cramped, bedroom upstairs is off-limits to you and your spacious bedroom will be off limits to me."

"Let's get one thing straight Marjorie. I don't bring women to this house and I don't want you bringing any strange men in here."

"What if they're not strange?" She laughed her shrill laugh again and Flint felt the cold chill grabbing at his spine.

"Any man. You go to his place or rent a motel, use his car or whatever. Screw him out on the lawn, but not in the house."

"I have no intention of taking up with any man at this time. I will get a job in Clarksburg, or wherever, and we can talk about you selling your half of this house to me or vice versa. Until then buddy boy, we will just live in harmony. Maybe, you'll want a piece of the action. I learned a few things you don't know, since I left you. Well, let me correct that, not a few, a lot. I made some comparisons to you Flint, and I must admit, you are the best. I really pity the women who go through life and don't make comparisons."

Flint didn't know if he should accept the compliment or not. He just looked at Marjorie with clenched jaws.

"Can I watch your television. I only watch the news and Hardball with Chris Matthews. Then you can have it after eight o'clock. Okay? It won't bother me if you watch the news with me."

Flint figured he would have to abandon the living room. He would be content with his bedroom and the spare room where he kept his hunting guns. His mind was in turmoil. Somehow he would have to get Marjorie out of the house permanently and get back to his comfortable lifestyle - Mavis on Wednesdays, and Michelle on Saturdays, militia meetings, his sheep in the field outside of the village and his job. His plate was a full platter. It could not hold much more.

13. Meeting at Earl's House

The arrangement with Marjorie would have been acceptable if she could only get her emotions and catlike behavior under control. Flint would ignore her most of the time they were in the house together. She would leave some left-over supper for him and he would eat it while she watched the evening news and Hardball. Basically, he kept out of her way and she kept out of his. Except for her flareups, their arrangement was accommodating. They bought their own food and respected that arrangement. If one of them desired something the other had purchased, for instance, red seedless grapes, they would ask permission to take some.

Marjorie would sometimes stay overnight somewhere unknown to Flint. He never questioned her on this matter and she never offered any explanation. There was no need to explain anything. They were lodgers in the house that they both owned. Somehow she still felt that she owned a piece of him. She tried to get him into an argument on their relationship, but Flint refused to participate with, "you leave me alone and I'll leave you alone." Once she went over to him while he was eating and tried to slap him. Flint grabbed her arm, pulled her toward the door, pushed her onto the porch and locked the door. She pounded on the door and made loud screams which was good entertainment for the neighbors, as well as hot news for the gossip mongers. These infrequent episodes often got back to Mavis.

It was Tuesday. Earl Hazzard scheduled a meeting at his house rather than at the old Grange Lodge. Flint thought he would walk the four miles from Buckeye to Chestnut, the patch where Earl lived. He needed to think. It would be about an hour walk there and an hour back. There was some snow on the ground and snow sifted lazily from the sky from time to time. He dressed warmly for the occasion and was about to start off when Marjorie asked him where he was going. He said, "I do not wish to discuss my activities with you." Her expression became grim. "Just trying to make inroads into the ice between us. There is no need for this antagonism."

It was seven o'clock and Earl's meeting was scheduled for

90

eight. Flint stepped out onto the porch and down the two steps to the walk and turned onto the narrow road that led from Buckeye to Hemlock. He passed the first house and at the bend in the road saw his image reflected in the darkened window. He noticed a figure outlined in the snow about a hundred feet behind him. He slowed to get a better image of the person behind him. There was no doubt that it was Marjorie tailing him.

Flint passed the last house in the patch, bent down to tie an imaginary shoelace and looked back to see if she was still there, following him. He walked slowly out onto the main road and headed toward Hemlock. The air was cold, but calm, and he was comfortable. He walked slowly until he was about a half mile from the last house. A quick look back certified that Marjorie was still following him. "Can't imagine why she would want to do that."

Halfway between the two patches he passed the sheep ranch and the house was well lit. Smoke was pouring from the chimney as if Ward Hollister had just built a fire in the fireplace. The smoke curled sideways about ten feet above the chimney and Flint thought about wind currents. He could imagine Ward and Miriam with their feet up on the coffee table watching television. The wool on the sheep would have grown back by now and the lambs would be well on their own.

After another half mile of walking a car came toward him, its headlights blinding him. When the car passed he turned and saw Marjorie had fallen behind by about a quarter mile. She was near the driveway to the sheep ranch. Flint increased his speed and didn't look back until he approached the first house in Hemlock. He turned when another car passed, but did not see his pursuer.

A meeting at the home of Earl Hazzard was always a feast of delicacies created by Mary, mistress of the house. Candied apple slices, fried squirrel legs, hot cider, whiskey, flavored biscuits, always something new. Mary was very creative and well liked by everyone. So was Earl for that matter, but he had an intensive dislike for the government. He had made a run for the West Virginia legislature about six years ago and was defeated. It was about the time Marjorie took off for Florida and he remembered the two events together. There was no connection between the two events, but that was the way Flint remembered them.

There were six members at the meeting, including Earl. Mary set out the food in what she called the gun room and disappeared. The Hazzard sons, Robert and Benny came in to say goodnight. Earl said that both of the boys were successful in hunting this year. Twelve year old Benny got a four point buck and ten year old Robert, a turkey. The members were indeed impressed and congratulated the boys each in their own way. Both boys bristled with pride.

Earl asked Robert to get his new turkey rifle and show it to the assembly. The boy was happy to do so as he hurried to his room and hurried back. The rifle was passed from one to the other. Flint put the rifle to his shoulder and aimed at the mounted deer head over the locked gun cabinet and took a mock shot. "This is a great gun for a kid your age. I could use something like this to hunt coyotes."

He went on to tell the others how he had called in a coyote at the sheep farm. Robert Hazzard asked Flint if he could go out with him the next time he called in coyotes and maybe he could be the one to shoot it. Flint liked Robert and said he would let him know when he was going out again. Maybe the militia would stage a coyote round-up and the entire hunting community could participate.

Flint was happy to see Jimmy Critchlow there and the pleasure was mutual. Elmer Atkins and Floyd Maynard, both close cohorts of Earl Hazzard were also in attendance. The other member was Alfie Solomon who had chosen to get into Flint's group at the rendezvous.

There was some informal banter and swigs of beer and whiskey before the meeting would get underway. Earl mentioned that Flint had missed the formal meeting last month and a couple of other informal meetings. Flint shook his head. "Ever since Marjorie came back, my life has been in turmoil. I decided to walk here and

92

she followed me, but I think she dropped off a mile back. She probably hitch hiked home." Most everyone chuckled at the way Flint told the story.

Earl asked Flint if he was still seeing the woman in Grafton. His love affair in Grafton was common knowledge to the inner circle, but not necessarily well known to everyone. Flint's response was, "Every Saturday night." "Why don't you marry her Flint?"

"Maybe, you don't remember, I'm already happily married." This brought down the house.

Earl said he would appreciate it if Flint attended all the meetings called. since he was second in command and was probably the smartest hillbilly in the area. Earl expected chuckles. Instead everyone nodded in agreement.

"How's things with Mavis Kramer, hear you've been calling on her." It was Floyd Maynard tossing out that grenade. He looked at Flint who already assumed that everyone heard the rumor.

Flint shrugged and sipped a little whiskey. "When Fred was shot I thought she needed another big brother and so I took Fred's tools to her and she said she appreciated my interest and said she wished I would visit her more often. We found out we both liked to play chess. So I see her and have been giving her advice."

"I'll bet," laughed Elmer. "I would like to advise her."

"No you wouldn't. She is an emotional anchor, ready to go off the deep end. Besides, she has a steady boyfriend now and nobody can cut into that scene. Billy wanted to marry her. After he went around bragging on how he knocked her up, he is lucky she didn't shoot him. She is good with the rifle you know. Took down several deer while she was still in high school."

"That boyfriend," mumbled Earl, "is he that Charlie the cop

93

who interviewed me?"

"Yeah, that's the one." Flint emphasized how much in love they were in order to take the heat off of himself and his relationship with Mavis. "At this point I'm willing to bet they will be married within two years.

Earl looked serious. His paranoia was well known. "Maybe, he is just trying to infiltrate our area and our organization to see just what Fred was up to."

"I don't think so." offered Flint. "I met the guy several times in the investigation and he is genuinely in love. He tries to give the impression he's just a country boy at heart, maybe so, but he is one shrewd country boy. He was raised over at West Union and his mother still lives there."

"Do you think Mavis is anxious to get even with that cop that shot Fred and this is her way of getting on the inside to get a crack at him." Earl had that squirrel look in his eyes that was familiar to those who knew him. When he had that look, you could assume there was intensity behind it.

"Naw, they are truly in love, but I do know that Mavis has sworn revenge on the person responsible for Fred's death." Flint suspected Earl had sent Fred on the mission and he was trying to get more information.

"Let's hope she gets her revenge," said Earl in all seriousness. "I'm certainly willing to help her in that endeavor." Flint smiled internally. He knew that the revenge would be against Earl and not the cop that shot Fred.

Earl said he was appalled by the number of people who were not willing to die for a cause. He said he would give his life to protect the constitution of the United States and the government was defiling that constitution. Would you guys be willing to die for some cause that is dear to your hearts? Everyone felt they would be willing to die if the cause was close and dear to them.

Earl talked as if the government of the country was not an elected body. He often referred to the government as the "Imperial Government. Elections were rigged to keep the Jews in power."

"You have to admire guys like Timothy McVeigh and David Koresh. They put their lives on the line for something they believed. By the way, that reminds me. Ray Pflipps has agreed to come back here and give a talk on the Oklahoma City bombing and maybe throw in a few comments on the event in Norway where the Norwegian patriot shot up a bunch of immigrants. I thought maybe invite him for February. Someone would have to put him up. Elmer did it before, but we can't ask him to do it again."

Jimmy looked at Flint and bit his lip. Flint gave him a knowing glance.

Elmer said he would talk to Alicia and he was sure she would agree to have Ray Pflipps back in their house. They did have the extra bedroom and Pflipps was no trouble the last time. Earl said he hoped Elmer would do that, but he hated to impose on him again. Earl was pleased that Pflipps had mentioned them in one of his broadcasts. In the broadcast he had thanked Earl for his leadership and Alicia and Elmer Atkins for their hospitality. He also talked about the militia and thought that other groups of listeners should organize likewise. He gave an address in Tennessee, where more information could be obtained.

Earl was on top of the situation. "Remember the last meeting with Ray Pflipps and how people had to listen to his message through the door and windows. Well, I was thinking of renting the Legion Hall in Salem. It's about a ten mile drive from our patches, but we probably could get a bigger attendance, especially if we advertised it. We could pass a can around for donations."

Flint rose and went to the bathroom across the hallway. As he lifted the toilet lid he noticed a folded Parkersburg newspaper on the back of the toilet. It was folded to an article about the shooting of a policeman on the river front that was still unsolved after two years. Much of the article was underlined with a pen. Surely, Earl Hazzard had nothing to do with this murder. The policeman had been investigating a series of burglaries at the time. Flint put the newspaper back in its original position and went back to the meeting.

There was a suggestion by Alfie Solomon that the militia have a camp-out in winter while the snow was still on the ground. They could bring sleeping bags and maybe portable tents, build cooking fires and experience some hardship just for the experience. Everyone thought that was a good idea and it would be a lot of fun. They agreed to a tentative date about a week after the next lecture by Ray Pflipps.

The refreshments were consumed. It was a little past ten and the meeting was generally over. Jimmy Critchlow told Flint he would give him a ride home if he wished, although he knew Flint enjoyed hiking in the snow, just as he did. Flint figured Jimmy had something on his mind and accepted the ride.

Jimmy drove slowly in order to extend the time. He asked Flint if he noticed Earl's eyes when he talked about Koresh and McVeigh. Flint said he hadn't. "Well, Flint, they were like burning coal embers embedded in the blackness of soot. That guy leans toward nutty. We have a lot of fun with our maneuvers, camp outs, meetings with snacks, but I think we have to watch out that we don't go over the brink."

"Earl reminds me of a squirrel hopping from one limb to another. Yeah, I think you're right about our keeping an eye on him. This is about the third time Earl mentioned my missing meetings and he wondered if I still had the interest in them. I told him that with

Marjorie at home now, I had a lot on my mind and she was interfering with my life too much. Actually, not too much, but I don't like having her around. We started talking about selling the house, but I thought we would get it appraised by the bank and I would take out a loan and pay her for her half of it. I don't really need a loan, since I don't spend my money foolishly. Maybe, finalize a divorce. I think she will go along with that."

14. The Wounded Warrior

Flint came home late from work on a Thursday evening, showered, got dressed and went for groceries at the Kroger store in Clarksburg. They had the best selection and the best prices of all the stores around. Most everyone in the patch communities shopped there. He ate a sandwich at Subway before heading back to the house.

It was shortly before nine when he arrived back in Buckeye. When he opened the door and walked in the kitchen he caught sight of Marjorie and some man in an embrace on the living room couch. They were illuminated by the glare of the television. He set his two bags on the kitchen table and went into the living room. He was set to throw both the man and Marjorie out. The man was Elmer Atkins. They parted when they heard Flint. When Flint saw the man was Elmer he relaxed.

"Dammit Marjorie, I told you we were not to have romantic guests in this house. I told you I would punch out any guy who you brought here and you were to warn them." He looked at Elmer. "Of course, Elmer, you are my friend, but I don't want any sexual activity in this house until Marjorie and I got things settled."

"Actually Flint, I came to see you and got to talking to Marjorie. We go back a ways, you know, friends in high school. We just hit it it off and were making other arrangements." He looked at Marjorie. She patted him on the leg.

97

"Tell you what Elmer. Why don't you two go to Marjorie's car and finish the discussion. I have to put away groceries and have some other chores. By the way, I didn't see your car in the parking area?"

Marjorie said that she ran into Elmer at the gas station in West Union and he said he had things to discuss with you so I brought him back with me. "I told him I would drive him back to his car."

Flint nodded his head. At this point Elmer was probably thinking about something that he could discuss with Flint in order to back up Marjorie's story. Flint didn't need any explanation. He saw the situation for what it was. "You know Elmer, if your discussion with Marjorie gets more intense, the Hillbilly Motel off Route 50 will rent you a room for ten bucks an hour."

"Where did you hear that Flint?" Elmer had a curious look on his face which broke into a grin.

"Let's just say that the word got around. You don't even have to sign in, and if you do sign in they don't care what name you put down. I understand George Washington stayed there a couple of times last week."

Marjorie rose, went to the hall closet and took out her coat. Elmer had left his on the floor of the small hallway. They never spoke to Flint as they exited the premises. Flint thought, *Elmer never did say what he wanted to see me about.*

It was a couple of weeks later when Flint was back at the Kroger store where he ran into Alicia Atkins who had a cart full of groceries. They greeted each other pleasantly. Alicia stated that Elmer seemed to be spending a lot of time at Flint's house lately. What did they talk about? Flint was blunt and said he resented Elmer using him as an alibi in order to bang Marjorie. Alicia agreed,

98

"I am not a stupid person Flint. I was being coy."

"I know you're not stupid Alicia. In fact you are probably the brainiest woman in these hills."

Alicia suggested they retaliate since their spouses were having an affair. Flint assured her he didn't think of Marjorie as his spouse and he didn't care what kind of social life she had. What did she mean by retaliate?

"You and I Flint, get it on together."

"Well Alicia, I think you are quite attractive and you look like you would be extraordinary good sex, I have to decline since my life is screwed up right now and I don't want it screwed up with some extra curricular activity. When I was approaching your cart, I was looking at your body and I was attracted by it, and here I go and find out it was you in those tight slacks. You really got a good body, as well as a pretty face."

"I guarantee you Flint, I would show you a very good time."

"I know you would Alicia. That's probably why Ray Pflipps figured out some excuse so he could come back here and get another piece of you. He is no more interested in this area and what our militia is doing than the man in the moon. It's you he's after. He's willing to drive all the way from Tennessee just to get a piece of you. Two thousand miles, you must really be good."

Alicia's serious expression broke into a grin. "You think so Flint."

"I would bet my life on it Alicia and if things straighten out for me, I'll take a rain check on your offer." He reached his hand out and patted her on the buttocks. "I really like the looks of that."

Larry Reynolds

Michelle Reynolds of Grafton was the lady that Flint stayed with every Saturday night. Flint missed a couple of Saturdays, but generally he felt wedded to Michelle. They were comfortable together and shared many of the same views. Every Saturday was like a vacation for them both. The sixty miles to her house always passed quickly as did the hour drive coming back home.

Larry Reynolds was the son of Michelle. She had him when she was eighteen years old. This age seemed to be a magic number for the women of rural West Virginia. The saying was that if you were a woman and weren't pregnant at eighteen, then you had a good life ahead of you. Larry was less than five years old when his father abandoned him and his mother. Now he was twenty two years old

Larry had joined the U.S. Marines when he finished high school. Flint had been on the scene for a couple of years before that time and Larry accepted him as a surrogate father and escort for his mother. He and Flint had worked together to put new roof shingles on the two story house. Flint also rewired most of the house with Larry at his side, learning the electric trade. Flint was twenty two years old when he built the house he now lived in.

The young marine had made it to grade E 5 when he was assigned to guard the Embassy in Iraq. Things went well there until one day a suicide bomber crashed into the barrier of the compound outside the Embassy. When a squad of marines went out to check the damage they were ambushed by a small group of Iraqis who were all killed in the battle. Unfortunately for Larry a bullet split his right kneecap in half and another bullet ripped through his left thigh and another through his stomach. The injury to his thigh and stomach did not have lasting consequences, but it would be a long time before the repair to his kneecap would allow him to walk again without a knee encased in a hard plastic shell.

When the rehabilitation advanced to the point where Larry could take care of his body he was given the option of going home to recuperate. There was an advanced rehabilitation facility for such injuries located in West Virginia at the Morgantown University

Hospital. Since Larry couldn't drive, the government would provide transportation from his home to Morgantown.

On Flint's second Saturday visit, Larry said that living at home was boring and he thought he might just go back to the military hospital where he and his fellow invalids could play cards and other games and engage in conversation.

Flint said that Morgantown was close enough to his neck of the woods. Why didn't Larry come home with him? It was Sunday and Flint would return him to his mother's house the following Saturday when he paid his usual visit. He hadn't exactly expressed it in those terms, but that was the idea. The driver of the rehab van that picked Larry up in Grafton could get him at Flint's house in the Buckeye patch instead of driving to Grafton. Larry made the call and everything was approved.

On the way home, Flint told Larry about Marjorie and gave him a pretty good idea of what to expect. It would be a break in the routine for Larry who could sleep until noon every day, watch television at night and Flint would drive him around and show him the sights before the sun went down. They would eat in a different restaurant every night.

Flint had moved the front seat of the pick-up as far back as it would go to accommodate Larry's leg which was in a stiff casing. The adjustable crutches were behind the front seat. The bags were in the rear of the truck.

Flint was surprised when Marjorie accepted Larry as a house guest without protest. She gave Larry a big welcome hug and sympathized with his leg.

Larry would sleep in Flint's bedroom on the ground floor and Flint would stay in what he called his den. Larry said he would be comfortable in the den and so Flint agreed to that arrangement. The small sofa in the den opened up into a single bed.

Things went well with this arrangement. Marjorie disappeared on Monday night and didn't return until Tuesday morning. The rehab van picked Larry up at ten a.m., and returned him just before sunset. Larry said the break in his routine was certainly welcome. Marjorie told Flint not to bother with restaurants every night, she would make a supper for her and Larry when Flint was pressed for time. Larry wondered why Flint and Marjorie were at odds, since they seemed to have a similar temperament, and he observed, a warm sentiment between them.

On Wednesday evening Flint said he had a meeting with a militia member and probably wouldn't be back until late. Of course, he was going to his Wednesday rendezvous with Mavis. Could Larry manage? Marjorie was within earshot. She said she had purchased some cheap CDs at the Walmart and if Larry was willing, they could watch them while Flint was gone. One was a western with Clint Eastwood and the other was a mystery featuring a vampire. Larry said he looked forward to the movies. Marjorie said she would make popcorn. She had a case of cold beer on the porch. It took too much room in the refrigerator, so she kept it on the porch.

Flint went to his rendezvous with Mavis. Between sexual episodes they discussed their present situations. Mavis worried that Charlie had a long way to drive on Saturdays and the gasoline must cost him a fortune. Flint said he identified with that because his drive to Grafton was also costly. Mavis hoped the trip and the expenses were worth it to Charlie. Flint assured her Charlie would drive across the country every weekend just to be with her. "That guy is hooked."

Mavis said she preferred to think of "in love" rather than hooked.

"Do you know any woman about your age who would be willing to go on a date with Larry? He's a real nice guy, but he seems to be without opportunity since he is tied up with the military. I thought you and Charlie could double date with some woman and Larry. Mavis said she would think about it and try to find some friend that wasn't tied up or in a serious romance."

Mavis told Flint about the previous Saturday. Charlie had arrived early. She was getting dressed while Charlie was feeding

Chloe before they took her over to Mildred. There was a knock on the door and before Charlie could get up, in walks Billy. He looked at Charlie who had a spoon in his hand and said, "Ain't that a nice family scene."

"I knew it was Billy and I rushed to the kitchen to avoid a confrontation. He was carrying a package. Naturally, I asked him what he was doing here. I didn't know he just walked in until Charlie told me later."

"That must have been unsettling, what did he want?"

"He said that Mildred had a bad cold and she didn't want to spread her germs to Chloe so she sent Billy over to babysit. He was dressed in work clothes, even though he doesn't work anywhere. I said that wasn't necessary and I didn't want Billy around Chloe under any circumstances. Charlie and I would stay at home in the evening, which is what we should have been doing right along. I hate to see Charlie buying me drinks at five dollars a pop."

"Did Billy leave quietly"

"No, he said something to Charlie about being the first guy to have me. Charlie's face tightened and I could see some anger building. Charlie was really holding back. I told Billy to leave and never come to this house again. If he had anything to deliver he could stand on the porch until I got there."

Mavis paused. Then continued. "Billy said that I was really slumming these days. I told him to get moving. He turned and headed for the door."

"Then what?"

"He turned and actually I could see his eyes were moist. He went over to Charlie at the table. I was beside Chloe who was in her high chair. I didn't know what would happen. Charlie was very alert.

Billy said, ' I'm sorry sir, please accept my apology. I didn't mean to be so shitty. It's just you two seem so happy together and I am terribly jealous.' Tears rolled down his cheeks."

"How did Charlie react?"

"He said he accepted the apology and would forget about what Billy had said, but it would be good if Billy never came around again. Then he told Billy they were hiring workers at the stone quarry in Bluefield and Billy could easily get a job there. West Virginia always gave preference to native sons when hiring workers."

"Billy said that was a two hundred mile commute. Charlie had to explain it to him. He wasn't supposed to commute, he was supposed to get a room around Bluefield and live there."

"Billy said he didn't want to leave the area and he would keep looking around. He was getting unemployment compensation, I don't know how he gets that, and he and Alfie Junior were sharing a flat in Salem. He just happened to be visiting his mother today. Probably to hit her up for some money because I hear he drinks a lot. I know he still smokes and cigarettes aren't cheap."

"All's well that ends well." smiled Flint. "So you stayed home, saved money, and still had a good time." Mavis kissed him on the cheek. "Yes we did."

The evening wasn't quite over for Flint. He got to his house around one thirty. Larry and Marjorie were both on the living room sofa watching television. Neither bothered to look up at him. There was an empty popcorn bowl on the coffee table and three empty beer bottles accompanying it. Larry's bum leg was stretched out along the side of the table.

"How was the movie?"

Larry said the first movie was great and this second one was just ending up. Marjorie said she was happy to have the company of such an interesting house guest. She actually got cold chills when Larry told her about the battle and how he was wounded. Flint said he had to get up early for work tomorrow and he shouldn't have stayed out so late, but he couldn't leave the meeting.

It was Thursday and the van picked up Larry as usual and transported him to the rehab center in Morgantown. He wouldn't get back until sunset if not after.

Flint came home, got cleaned up, sat down for his quick microwave supper. He was halfway through it when Marjorie came through the door, stood in a pose that suggested the start of a dance, decided not to do the dance, then headed for a seat at the table.

After she was settled, Flint thanked her for entertaining Larry for the evening. Marjorie said it was the other way around, he entertained her. She smiled. It was a smile that Flint had recognized as one that inferred the cat had swallowed the canary.

"Okay, how about telling me how it went with Larry."

Marjorie poured herself two inches of scotch and sat down at the table with Flint. "The first movie was a romantic comedy with a lot of bare skin and sexual innuendo. It wasn't Clint Eastwood. I said it was making me romantic and went to kiss your little buddy Larry. He refused my advance. I said why not, we were adults and alone. He mumbled something about exchanging body fluids and he didn't know me well enough to do that. I figured you must have told him I had some kind of disease. Did you?"

"I mentioned that you sleep around a lot and any guy that associated with you will have associated with many other men. That's true isn't it."

"Yeah, I guess so. To some extent. Not different guys. Only

two at this time. But, I assure you I do not have any disease. I had a bad internal rash a year or so ago but antibiotics cleared that up and I am clean now."

"I'll take your word for it. Please continue. I'm all ears. Was that it?"

"No, I kept my hand on his leg and kept rubbing it. He didn't object. I put my head into his chest and looked up. He kissed me on the neck. I figured that was a good cue so I zipped down his fly and . said he could put it in me. He said his bad leg prevented that. He started feeling my boobs through the sweater, so I exposed them and he kissed them passionately. I liked that and continued fondling him.. I was ready with the tissue and caught it before it got splattered all over the place. I know how fussy you would be if there was strange fluids all over the floor."

"Sounds like you did entertain him. Very interesting. Was that it?"

"Yeah, I guess that was it except for some boob kissing. He was worried that you might show up any minute or I might have given it a second go. He swore me to secrecy, so please don't tell him that I told you."

Flint said, "My lips are sealed."

"Okay George. The kid was fascinated by my boobs and kept kissing them. I do have great boobs." She unfastened her shirt, there was no bra and her boobs were exactly as the billing of them promised. Firm, fully blown, not the least sag. They were superior to a Greek statue.

Flint was tempted to reach out a hand and feel them, but he didn't want to take a chance on how he would react. "I have no reason to doubt what you told me is true, knowing you. Tell you

106

what. He goes back home with me on Saturday. I'll disappear on Friday night and you can treat him one more time."

"I have other arrangements on Friday evening. Maybe, I'll get him tomorrow afternoon while you're at work and maybe get a little more involved."

She waited to see how Flint would react. She was disappointed. He didn't react.

15. Camp Out In December

Days get shorter as well as colder in mid-December. Earl Hazzard decided that the militia would camp out on Camp Mistake Hill in the yard of the abandoned building that they had shot up on their recent maneuvers. That event went very well with timing and coordination and Earl was very pleased with it. He was also very pleased with his leadership which he was certain everyone admired. The leadership had little to do with the pleasure of the firing range, hunting, and now camping out. There was also a raft trip planned for the flood waters of the Kanawha River in April or May.

They would park their vehicles at the base of the old logging road and hike up to the abandoned house, set up camp, cook their meal over a Coleman stove or perhaps over the open fire, sleep in their sleeping bags, and maybe practice shooting.

The thermometer on the porch post read 24 degrees Fahrenheit at the home of Jimmy Critchlow when Sophie invited Flint in to have a cup of hot coffee before they got started. The three of them were sitting at the table when Flint made a casual remark about Ray Pflipps being at the maneuvers. Sophie said she was surprised that he didn't move to the hills considering his affair with Alicia Atkins. Jimmy had told Sophie that he had told Flint and they all agreed to keep that information to themselves. Sophie asked Flint if he would like to see the stage where the performance took place. He said he certainly would and regretted he had not been part of the audience. Sophie assured him it was a good show.

She led Flint into her bedroom that overlooked the Atkins home down below. There were binoculars on the window sill. The glare on the windows below made it difficult to see inside the Atkin's house. Sophie handed the binoculars to Flint and said look in the window on the right. Flint did and saw the living room with perfect clarity. Sitting on the sofa was Elmer Atkins dressed in a camo outfit and having a cup of coffee. There was a plate of doughnuts in front of him.

"Very good view." He handed the binoculars back to Sophie who put them back on the window sill.

"I hear Ray Pflipps is coming back to town. Maybe, I'll invite you over for the show."

Jimmy interrupted with a laugh. "I don't know if I want you and Flint in the same bedroom watching a porno show."

Flint and Jimmy arrived at the base of the hill where they waited for the other guys to show up. In about fifteen minutes there were eight men walking up the old road with backpacks. Five of them also had rifles strapped to the packs. The three without rifles were Earl Hazzard, Elmer Atkins, and Floyd Maynard. Flint assumed the three, who were close friends, had decided to carry handguns instead of their rifles. Handguns were a sign of the officer class in the military.

Elmer thought they should set up a kitchen in the old house, but was overruled by Earl who said that they should get an outside experience. In a combat situation the last place you would want to be is in an isolated abandoned house. When the enemy approached and saw the house you would never leave it alive, unless you surrendered. Nobody challenged that assessment. However, Flint said he would sleep in the house and he didn't want anyone firing shots into it. He thought to make a joke. "If the enemy arrived, it would have red hair." There were a few grins, but nobody laughed.

It was Alfie's opinion they should get some training setting up a perimeter around the house and protecting it. Elmer thought that was a good idea. Earl said, "Some other time."

Snow was tramped down in a ten foot circle. Some old building stones were brought to the stomped area and a fire circle was made. Most everyone went foraging for firewood and a good supply was quickly found. There were many trees down and the limbs were easily broken from the older ones. Jimmy brought loose boards from the front of the house. He thought he would make himself a lean-to shelter for the night, but on second thought, decided to add them to the pile of firewood that was accumulating.

Earl had a wire shelf from an old oven. He set it up on three stones, and built a small fire under it. This would be the cooking fire that would accompany the camp fire. Alfie mumbled "White man build big fire, sit back, Indian build small fire, sit close." They had all heard it before so there was just acceptance and no comment. The Coleman stove would be used if the grate was not adequate.

Once the cooking fire had settled down to a small size, Earl put a sheet of aluminum foil on the wire screen and a few small stones to hold it in place while he cut open two packs of sausage links and spread them on the wire grill. He covered these with another layer of aluminum foil held down with stones that were exposed on the ground where the snow had melted. Earl brought the sausage and Coach brought the buns. Alfie, Dan and Floyd were already drinking beer. Each of them had brought a twelve pack which they intended to share with the others. Their backpacks would be much lighter on the way down the hill.

Flint provided a small gallon sized cooking pan. Jimmy had a small eight cup coffee pot that would be in constant use. Everyone had his assignment given by Dan who was good at organization. If everyone did his assignment, things would go smoothly. They would eat, drink, hike and sleep. Good thing Alfie brought two rolls of toilet paper and an area over by the trees was designated for that activity. Ordinarily a slit trench would be dug and put in use, but the ground was frozen solid and anyway the weather would disintegrate any feces and toilet paper left about.

It was noon before everything was in the condition desired. During the day the men would go off in pairs to reconnoiter. They were given assignments to walk to the road surrounding the hill and back again. They all had compasses. Flint and Jimmy would go north. Alfie and Dan would go south, Earl and Elmer would go east, Coach and Floyd would go west. They would leave at hour intervals. The last group of Coach and Floyd would probably be returning after the sun had set. They would carry flashlights. No need to emphasize that, since everyone had a flashlight.

Flint and Jimmy were the first to go out and they duly headed north. They walked along the ridge which trended north - south and was on part of a hiking trail. When the trail shifted off their intended direction they followed their compass and began going downhill, some of which was very steep. They came to the rock wall which seemed to follow the trend of the ridge and were able to climb down it without difficulty. At the base of the wall they found a cave that receded into the rock for about six feet before it turned into a large crevice. "We should have set up camp here." offered Jimmy.

"Probably some raccoons back in that crevice. Maybe we should get one and take it back to eat."

Flint said to keep going and get this over with. "I don't mean I'm not enjoying this. This is my kind of fun, much better than television and sex." He looked at Jimmy and laughed.

"Don't say its more fun than sex, you know better than that." He used the old phrase, "even when it's bad, it's still pretty good."

As Flint and Jimmy approached the base of the hill they came to a cabin about fifty yards in front of them. There was smoke coming out of the chimney. Flint stopped. "I guess this is where we turn around, we are almost at the bottom. How long have we been out?"

Jimmy removed the glove on his left hand and pushed that sleeve back with his gloved right hand. "We've been on the trail for just over forty five minutes."

"Then we will be back at camp by two o'clock. Just in time for a beer and a sausage. I have six hard boiled eggs that I'll share with you. I even brought packets of salt and pepper that I stole from Arbys."

It was slightly after two o'clock when they arrived back at camp. Alfie and Dan were gone, and Earl and Elmer were just leaving. Coach and Floyd were eating and apparently still gathering firewood which was now piled about six feet high. The pile would easily last throughout the night if someone wanted to feed the fire.

There was a shot coming from the east. It was not a rifle shot. Coach remarked that was where Elmer and Earl were headed and they both carried pistols. Rather than try to investigate they would just wait and hear the story about that shot.

When Elmer and Earl returned, Elmer was carrying a dead possum. Earl shot it with his handgun and so Elmer was duty bound to carry it. "Earl plinked this guy at about sixty feet. What a shot. Most of the possum was behind a limb on the tree."

Alfie said he would field dress it and get the best parts on the fire as soon as possible. They would enjoy a taste of possum before bedtime. He would slather it with mustard before he put it on the coals over of the cooking fire ashes after the aluminum foil was removed from the grill.

The last two men, Coach and Floyd, must have cut their trip short since it was still daylight when they returned. The sun was almost down and everyone was assembled. There were a lot of beer cans around and these were set up in front of the foundation of the building. Earl, Elmer, and Floyd were first to fire since they had pistols. They were at a distance of fifty feet and each emptied a clip into the cans.

After that shooting was complete the others examined the pistols. Earl had a 9 millimeter pistol. Floyd's was a 32 caliber and Elmer's was a twenty two long. Earl also had a smaller automatic hand gun that was a 22 long caliber, similar to Elmer's. He said the trouble with the 22 automatic was that the long bullets were too long and the gun jammed. If he used a shorter bullet then the automatic worked well.

It was the riflemen's turn. They stood in a line about a hundred feet from the building. The cans were reset and in the fading sunlight they each emptied ten rounds into the cans. Flint remarked to Coach. "That just cost me ten bucks." There followed a serious discussion about where one could purchase the cheapest ammunition. Coach said he reloaded his ammo. He picked up his empty shell casings as well as those of several of the others.

They sat around the fire consuming coffee and beer. Flint dunked a tea bag in his cup containing hot water which had the taste of burned wood in it. He took some ribbing for drinking tea even though he explained it made him sleep better. Earl had a flask of whiskey which he passed around and everyone drank from it. Floyd said he hated to drink after Elmer cause "God only knows where his lips have been." It was a good joke, but Flint didn't laugh. He wondered if any of the others knew about Elmer and Marjorie. Elmer laughed, took a drink, then passed the flask on to Coach.

It was ten o'clock and everyone agreed it was time to bed down for the night. They spread out their sleeping bags, put their boots in plastic bags and crawled into their sacks. Flint took his sleeping bag

112

to the house and with his flashlight made his way to the room that he had examined earlier in the day. It was the room that the hiker had used when they almost shot off his head. It had snow around the edges, but the center was bare. He kicked away a small tree limb that had somehow found its way into the building.

Flint lay in his sleeping bag and thought about the recent events. It was Saturday night and he would miss the stay-over with Michelle. She seemed to be losing interest in him and didn't complain when he said he was going camping with his militia buddies. She was six years older than him and made remarks to that effect several times. Flint assured her it was not a great age discrepancy and they did very well together, which they both knew was a true statement. But, he mused, they probably had exhausted their relationship of the energy and glow it once had. He really would like to have Mavis on a regular basis and in full view of the community.

He thought about Mavis and her beau Charlie, the cop. If there was ever a pair that was matched in Heaven they were it. He was upset when Mavis decided to call off their usual Wednesday night fling, but he reasoned that Mavis could not take a chance on losing Charles Fitch, officer of the law. Mavis would be starting classes at Clarksburg University in the new year and she certainly didn't need Flint complicating her life.

Then there was wild-ass Marjorie who muddled his emotions. They once had a lot of fun and excitement together. He thought about the time they stood nude under the waterfall at Blackwater State Park. They had been married three years. When she turned thirty, he thought, something had gone wrong in her brain and she decided to leave him. Whatever it was that had gone wrong in the brain it seemed to be righting itself at this time and she was appearing normal again. He wasn't going to take any chances. He had invested too much emotion into his marriage and relationship and he wasn't going to go through that again. Up until that time, Marjorie was the only women with whom he had a sexual relationship. He reached in his back pack and took out a small bottle of scotch whiskey and drank half its contents. He looked at his boots that were on the side of his backpack and hoped some animal didn't run off with them during the night. He reached over and tied the laces together in order to make it harder for any animal to cart them off. Then, he put his head on the little pillow that came with the sleeping bag, zipped up the bag over his head and went to sleep.

Flint rose just as the sun was coming up. He dressed and went to the fire, but alas it had gone out and the area was covered with a new six inch layer of snow. The seven men in the sleeping bags were all covered with the newly fallen snow. He went to the camp fire which was the only place not covered with snow and stirred the ashes. Down underneath there was some heat and when he stirred it there was a curl of smoke. He knelt down and blew on the ashes. Soon there was a small flame. He extracted a tissue from his pocket and put it on the flame, then he broke small gray twigs from one of the limbs they had dragged in the day before. Soon he had a respectable fire going. And soon after that, the men began emerging from the sleeping bags and shaking the snow from them.

There was coffee and biscuits warmed on the cooking grill. Coach brought out a box of store-bought doughnuts. Floyd held up the box, looked at Coach and laughed. "Aren't we the fancy one."

16. January

The days moved quickly and Mavis started college classes at Clarksburg University. She was given a Tuesday and Thursday schedule of three classes and a fourth class that was an internet course on English Literature. She made arrangements for Mildred to take care of Chloe on the days she would be at the university. Charlie would still be making the 150 mile trip from Charleston every Saturday. He no longer stayed at his mother's in West Union, but stayed with Mavis. More often, than not, they would simply stay home and watch television as well as engage in pleasurable pursuits. They kept Chloe at home when they weren't going anywhere.

114

Mildred said she would prefer to have Chloe stay overnight with her even if Mavis and Charlie were not going out.

Charlie took Mavis and Chloe to West Union to meet his mother and sister. The meeting went exceptionally well. His mother held Chloe on her lap the entire time and it appeared she would never release her. Chloe obliged by sitting peacefully and listening to the conversation.

As luck would have it, January 16 was on a Saturday. It was Chloe's second birthday and a small gathering would celebrate it. Flint was invited and he could bring Michelle if he wanted to. He thought that Michelle didn't know any of the Buckeye people so he made her the offer and talked her out of going. She would be content to stay at home with her son Larry while George attended the birthday party. Michelle never referred to him as Flint.

Mavis and Flint agreed to end their intimate relationship. She didn't want to take a chance on losing Charlie. Flint said he understood. He would now consider Mavis to be the younger sister he never had and he would be the unacknowledged godfather of Chloe. When Flint mentioned that idea, Mavis said, "Don't think of me as your sister, think of me as your friend. I might want some more of you in the future and I don't want to think of you as my brother, only as a friend of my brother."

There were only a few people at the party which featured a cake with two candles and several wrapped presents. Millie was there. She pumped Flint for as much gossip as she could get. Flint hinted there was a rumor that Alicia Atkins and the rabble rousing radio personality Ray Pflipps had got it on when he was here and stayed at the Atkins house. Mildred said that it was old news and she was skeptical about it. She whispered, "Alicia is too attractive to settle for a spectacle like Ray Pflipps." Flint said sometimes people get desperate for adventure.

The small gathering included a young woman named Jane

Rendell whom Mavis had met at the university. Jane was a year older than Mavis and they had known each other briefly in high school. Flint watched Jane closely and she could feel Flint's eyes upon her. Why didn't Flint concentrate on Millie, wondered Jane. Millie was attractive, slim build, with well kept light brown hair tinged with gray. Only a few years, well more than a few years, older than Flint. The concentration on Jane by Flint was more of curiosity than romantic. Perhaps she would be interested in meeting Larry?

Everyone was in the kitchen. There was the singing of happy birthday and the blowing out the candle ceremony. It took Chloe two tries. Millie explained that the song happy birthday was originally written by a school teacher and the song was first titled "Good Morning Dear Teacher." She sung the original version "Good morning dear teacher, good morning dear teacher, we're all in our places, with sun shiny faces, good morning dear teacher, good morning to you." Her effort was met with smiles.

Flint presented Chloe with a plastic tricycle he had left on the porch. It could be ridden around the kitchen and maybe outdoors. The unpaved road of Buckeye would be a challenge for those little legs. It was the thought that counted. Chloe was given instruction on the trike, but it was not yet something she wanted to do. She wanted more cake.

As the party was winding down Mavis said she had a surprise. Everyone was to stay in the kitchen and sit tight while she went into the bedroom. Everyone agreed to sit tight.

A few minutes later, the word "boo" was heard and a bear's head popped around the doorway. Everyone was at attention. Then Mavis in a bear costume jumped out and said, "Ta -ta." There was a lot of chuckling. Chloe raised her hands over her head and exposed a face full of blue cake icing.

When the initial reaction had subsided Mavis removed the bear head from her own head. "How do you like it?"

Flint asked, "What's this all about? It's not Halloween."

Mavis explained. As a part of her tuition scholarship, she would be the team mascot for the Clarksburg Bears. She would be at the Tuesday and Thursday basketball games when they played at home and football games in the fall. There might also be some parades and civic functions that she could attend if she wanted to be there with the university band. She would be paid thirty dollars for each game she attended. She would not have to report this income to public assistance since it was travel expense reimbursement. She had to compete against four other acrobats for the job.

All congratulated her and thought it would be a lot of fun. Mavis said she would give Millie the thirty dollars for baby sitting. Millie said she wasn't baby sitting since it was her grandchild and she would gladly take Chloe into her home permanently any time Mavis was willing. This brought a sober reaction from those in the kitchen.

Chloe wanted down. Charlie wiped her face and hands and plucked her out of the high chair. He kissed her several times as he placed her on the floor. Millie wanted to, but could not prevent the eruption of a smile on her face as she watched Charlie and his affection for Chloe.

The plastic tricycle, or was it a cart, was brought out again and Chloe was fitted into it. Her attempts to get it going were not good. Flint gave it a little push and Chloe was able to go from the kitchen into the living room where she rammed it into the sofa because she didn't know how to turn around.

There would be a gathering at the university gymnasium on Martin Luther King Holiday, which of course, was on a Monday. All government and state offices were shut down. The university band would be playing and several speeches would be made, one by the governor. Mavis would be there in her bear costume. Flint took the day off from work in order to see her in action. Not everyone was released from work on federal and state holidays.

There were about two hundred people in the gymnasium

117

where only one side of the stands was open to seating. This faced the small stage erected in the center of the gymnasium floor where dignitaries were already seated. Flint had made his way to the top row of the seats. He noticed Earl Hazzard, wife Mary and the two boys Benny and Robert about ten rows in front of him. Benny looked around and saw Flint. He then told the others that Flint was there. They turned their heads in unison.

It was only a matter of seconds when Earl excused himself from his family and went to sit next to Flint. He said he didn't know Flint was coming or he would have given Flint a ride to the event. Why was Flint here? Flint said he wanted to see Mavis performing in her bear mascot uniform. Earl marveled at that and had a lot of questions about Mavis and said he would go down and tell his family about Mavis Kramer being the bear mascot and then he would be right back.

Why was Earl at the gathering? He wanted to get Mary and the kids out of the house as cheaply as possible and this was a good time. He also wanted to get a good look at the governor and his circle of friends. Since they were almost alone on the upper bench Earl said, "you know, it would be an easy shot to pick off the

governor from here." Flint said that was a strange comment. Earl offered that it wasn't strange, it was just something that came to mind.

There was a drum roll and Mavis in her bear costume entered from a side door doing cartwheels and hand jumps. Then she straightened up and waved her arms and moved forward with great hip twisting vigor as the band played a loud rendition of *Stars and Stripes Forever*. Mavis led them around the gym floor. They played until the number was over, then took seats at the side of the stage. The drummers were in the front row and had put their drums in front of them. They would give a drum roll and Mavis did some gyrations. Flint thought about those moving hips. He couldn't help smiling because he knew there was a great female body inside that bear skin. His mind did not wish to underplay the pretty face that invited kissing.

The mayor of Clarksburg rose, went to the microphone, looked at the band and Mavis, made some compliment and then looked at the audience. "Will you please rise for the playing and singing of the national anthem. Everyone seemed to be up. A strong voiced male singer began. Flint looked at Earl who was very slow to rise. "I don't know Flint, if I want to be on my feet or not." "It's a courtesy to all the heroes of America." "Well, Martin Luther King wasn't one of them."

When the anthem was over and everyone was seated, the mayor started giving a speech with a sheet of paper in front of him on the podium. Earl shuffled. He wasn't listening to the mayor. Neither was Flint for that matter. Earl leaned closer to Flint. "I think Ronald Reagan was our greatest president who didn't make mistakes. However, he made a big one in creating "boogie man national holiday." Flint didn't acknowledge the remark. Pretended he was listening to the blather the mayor was dispensing. Wished Earl was not there. He wanted to concentrate on the bear and think about the beautiful face and body that was underneath the costume.

The mayor ended his part of the program. The band would play *America the Beautiful* and the singer once again asked the audience to sing along. To Flint's surprise Earl sang along. He had a very nice singing voice. When Flint complimented Earl he answered that he enjoyed singing and playing the banjo. "Maybe you could play the banjo at one of our meetings." Earl answered, "I don't want our meetings to be entertaining."

The governor gave his talk. He tried to be witty, but his wit fell on ears not accustomed to political humor. There was a long presentation concerning why Martin Luther King was honored and how he changed American history. MLK was honored by having his portrait on the stamps of more than fifty countries of the world. Earl leaned again, "Yeah, all of them in Africa."

There was a child making noises off to the left. The mother of the child picked it up, started down the steps. It wasn't the mother, it was the grandmother and the child was Chloe. Flint wanted to join them, but he decided it would only be more of a disturbance if people started leaving the audience. He would be content to sit through the ceremony and listen to the barbs of Earl Hazzard.

When the ceremonies were ending, the band played *Stars and Stripes Forever* with Mavis doing her thing. They exited from the gymnasium through the door that they had entered.

Flint went down and said hello to Mary and the boys, then hurried out to the reception hallway, but he could not find Mavis or Millie.

17. February

February had come on the scene with a ten inch snowfall. Many chimneys were belching smoke produced by wood burning furnaces and fireplaces despite most people in the area being connected to the gas wells that served for underground storage. Those that owned large tracts of land received free gas while those in the patches had meters. One of the jobs that the gas workers rotated was to read the meters. Flint didn't mind it when it was his turn to read the meters. He was often invited into homes for a cup of coffee when he made his rounds. He would often get a piece of pie along with the coffee and, of course, the gossip of the week. There was opportunity for sex in that set-up, but Flint never pursued that line of thought. He was not aggressive where sex was concerned and he felt out-of-place when he thought about it with just any woman.

Earl invited Flint and Floyd Maynard to his house and told the other members of the militia that they were going to have a special session and the membership would be informed as to the outcome of it at the next meeting at the end of the month. This was not true, the other members would not be told what Earl had in mind.

Flint was surprised when he saw that he was only one of three in attendance. He felt uneasy about the meeting when he phoned Jimmy in order to pick him up and was informed that Jimmy was not invited. He asked Earl for an explanation. Earl said that the explanation would be given shortly. Wife Mary made the usual snacks and retired from the gun room.

Earl began by saying that he trusted Flint and Floyd to be discreet and not reveal what is said here to anyone. They agreed to that.

The captain of the Mountaineer Militia looked at Flint. "How serious is Mavis Kramer about getting even with the person who killed her brother?" Flint wondered what Earl had in mind then he said he thought she was very serious.

Earl said there would be a big celebration in Parkersburg on St. Patrick's Day. The guest of honor would be the Secretary of State who is a friend of the governor. Also at the celebration would be one of the U.S. Senators from the state, a U.S. Representative, the mayor and a lot of other dignitaries. "The Clarksburg University band will be there. If we could get Mavis Kramer to wear a bomb under her bear costume, she could move up to the platform and blow them all to smithereens."

The guy must really be crazy, thought Flint. "How do you think you could get Mavis to go along with that scheme? I'm sure she wouldn't want to kill herself. She has a child to care for."

"I thought about that. We could convince her that she would be avenging the death of her brother and doing the country a favor. Her name would be immortal. Millie would raise the child."

"I don't know Earl, that's asking a lot of a person."

Floyd Maynard didn't seem to be surprised by the proposal.

121

He had an opinion. "We could sweeten the pot by setting up a fund for the orphan. Maybe a hundred grand. Everyone is gonna die sometime and why not die for a good cause?"

Earl said that he could get a lot of money for the project from a source he would not name. Flint pretended to go along with the project. He now had every intention of scuttling it and getting revenge on Earl who had obviously put Fred up to his ill fated mission. "Why not get somebody to wear an explosive device, run up to the stage, and do the job." He wasn't serious, but threw that possibility out anyway.

Earl was ready for the question. "Because security would be tight. No one would search the band and the mascot. They would be given a pass. Everyone else at the ceremony would be under scrutiny. The band from Marshall University will also be there along with their mascot, which I think is a duck or something like that. It would be perfect."

"Yes, if we could convince Mavis." Flint was really upset and struggled not to show it.

"I know you and Mavis are close Flint, ever since Fred was killed by the government, and I was hoping you would talk to her and convince her it is a patriotic duty."

"Well, we are close and I am the unofficial godfather of Chloe."

"Let's be up front Flint. You were seen leaving her house at some very odd hours in the evening several times."

"Yes, that's true. We often play chess and she still needs consoling. She has her boyfriend, but he doesn't know our community well enough to give her the comfort she needs. After all, her brother was shot by the police under some suspicious

122

circumstances, and he represents the police."

"Yeah, consoling," said Floyd Maynard with a laugh.

"Don't push it Floyd." warned Flint. Maynard apologized and said it was a reflex action and would be funny under different circumstances. Flint accepted that and said he understood the joke and agreed it would be funny under different circumstances.

Earl wanted to know if Flint would feel Mavis out and get her to a meeting with him, Flint, and Floyd. Flint said Jimmy Critchlow had the same mindset as himself and wondered if Jimmy could be in on the plan. If Mavis agreed to meet with them, then it might be a good idea to have Jimmy along because Jimmy was actually a closer friend of Fred's than he was and Jimmy is related to Mavis by blood. Actually, Flint wanted Jimmy along as back up to his treachery.

Earl looked at Floyd. "What do you think of cutting Jimmy in on this?"

"If Flint vouches for him, I think it would be okay."

"Okay Flint, feel out Mavis and if she seems agreeable, then contact me and we will set up a meeting and maybe, I say maybe, invite Jimmy to come along. This is my idea and I want to direct it from start to finish."

The meeting was over. Flint would talk to Mavis and get back to Earl. He might also talk to Jimmy who once expressed the opinion that Earl should be locked up in jail or at least in a crazy house.

As Flint drove home he thought of a phrase Winston Churchill once uttered, "Three people can keep a secret, if two of them are dead."

When Flint approached Mavis with the idea of blowing herself up to avenge her brother's death Mavis was stunned and after a few minutes on the verge of hysteria. Flint laughed and said that it was out of the question of course, but somehow the idea could be used to destroy Earl's influence on his fellow mountaineers and maybe disgrace him with the community who seemed to hold him in high esteem. Maybe there could be a pay-off for Mavis in all of this.

There was nothing wrong with getting back at Earl, but even the suggestion was dangerous. She really despised that man and would certainly like to get him somehow.

They discussed the situation for a long time. Flint said that Earl was willing to pay Mavis a large sum of money if she would go along with the deal. The money could be put in a trust fund for Chloe. Mavis was now interested. "How much money?"

"Surely, you're not considering it?"

"Of course not, I don't want to blow myself up, but I was thinking maybe I could con him out of some money. How much do you think he would offer? If things got rough I am willing to testify that Fred told me he was put up to the assassination by Earl and that if I ever needed help I could go to Earl. When I went to Earl after the event he was oh so sorry that Fred had been killed, he thought they should have just arrested him."

Flint thought a while. "If you are serious you could pretend to go along with it and have Earl get you the money in advance, deposit it in some account and then at the last minute back out of the deal. You would have the money and there would be no way for him to get it back. The money would probably come from his contacts and they would certainly not expose themselves."

Mavis thought that Earl was capable of severe retaliation and she would be in danger. She didn't like his narrow squirrel eyes. Flint thought they could pull it off and if Earl was threatening Mavis or Chloe, he Flint, would shoot him and take the consequences. But he would like to see Earl dishonored and maybe jailed with some charge of conspiracy to commit murder.

Mavis was so intent on getting back at Earl for what he did to Fred she was willing to risk it knowing that Chloe would be well cared for by Millie. She might even be a better mother to Chloe than she was. Flint said that he would have Jimmy Critchlow to back them up in the scheme. He would inform Jimmy in advance of the details.

"Why have Jimmy involved."

"Jimmy has personal reasons for disliking Earl. Jimmy was Fred's best friend and he suspected Earl put Fred up to it, even though Fred never indicated to Jimmy that he was going to do something horrendous. Another thing, Earl is always making disparaging remarks about Jews and Sophie's parents are both Jews."

"You're kidding Flint. I didn't know."

"Well why should you? We are all Americans and there's no need to discuss our heritage with anybody."

The meeting was set up in the back room of the Mountaineer Restaurant. Mavis had ridden to the meeting with Flint. Those present were Earl Hazzard, Floyd Maynard, Jimmy Critchlow, George "Flint" Haloway and Mavis Kramer. Earl was dressed in an expensive blue business suit. The others were in their daily attire.

Earl was in control of the meeting and relished his role. He outlined to Mavis the plan. "He would get an explosive jacket made to fit Mavis under her bear costume. There would be an easy activating device that would blow out about thirty feet. During the parade Mavis could pretend to be doing cute tricks. She would go up to the stand where the Secretary of State would be and blow them all up.

"Including me," said Mavis with a voice of depression.

"Yes," said Earl with enthusiasm, "and your name would go

down in history along with David Koresh and Timothy McVeigh. You would be famous world-wide."

Floyd Maynard added. "We would build a twenty foot high memorial to you right up near our meeting headquarters."

Flint looked at Jimmy and moved his head slightly as if to say, how about that.

Earl could hardly contain himself. "It would be one of the greatest events in the history of retaliation against our oppressive government."

"I don't know," offered Mavis. "The government has been pretty good to me. They gave me assistance when I needed it. They"re giving me a scholarship to the university. The government has treated me very well."

It was a detour from the road Earl had planned. "Think of Fred. You want to get back at the people who killed him, don't you?"

"I certainly would like to get back at the person responsible for Fred's death."

Earl didn't realize that Mavis meant him. "And you can avenge your brother's death, by doing this. And it would make you famous."

It came time for Mavis to make her move. "What's in it for me beside revenge and fame?"

The captain of the militia thought he had scored. "We will give you enough money to set up a trust fund for your daughter. It will be more than enough to carry her into old age. Besides, her grandmother Millie has made no bones about wanting to raise the girl on her own. She would be a fine person to raise Chloe."

"I agree, Millie would be great at raising Chloe." She paused and looked seriously at Earl. "How much money are we talking?"

"How about two hundred thousand dollars?"

Mavis thought for about a minute. She looked perplexed. "If Chloe spent twenty thousand a year, that would only last ten years. That's not enough for the task involved."

Earl gulped. "What figure would you have in mind?"

"When Flint told me about this meeting, I thought about it. How about a half million dollars?"

"Would you do it for a half million?"

"I believe I would, but the money would have to be in my account long before St. Patrick's Day. If the parade and ceremony was called off I intend to keep the money."

"Only fair," choked Earl. "Only fair. But you could still earn the money if we gave you another assignment."

Mavis asked how the money would get to her. Earl said he would have to clear the amount with someone he wouldn't name and he would give her the details later. He thought that the money would arrive by UPS and she would have to sign for it. The money would be in a box with several types of wrapping. She would be able to deposit the money or do with it whatever she wanted before St. Patrick's Day. There might be a problem with so large an amount in cash, but Mavis could think about an explanation for it, like she found it in a trunk that belonged to her mother and father, or something like that.

Mavis said it was a deal. She would only see Earl again when she went to pick up the bomb jacket and an explanation on how to detonate it. She would find out when the band bus would leave for Parkersburg and inform Earl of the time so they could work out the details. Maybe Flint or someone could drive her to Clarksburg to get on the team bus. Flint said he would do it.

"I was at the last basketball game Mavis," said Earl with intensity in his voice. "I noticed a nigger hugging the bear. What was that all about?"

Mavis forced a smile. She looked at Flint and then at Floyd. "Clarksburg has three black players. I don't know them. In fact, I don't know anyone on the team. I just do my job. Anyway, this black guy, I think his name is Ernie scored a basket just before the buzzer and I was standing along the wall near the hoop. He rushed over, picked me up and swirled me around. When he picked me up his hands were on my boobs. He put me down and had the strangest expression. He said, honest I didn't know you wuz a woman, I thought you wuz some college guy. He kept standing there and apologizing. The coach hollered at him to get back in the game. That was that."

"Those Africans don't know there place." murmured Earl.

"Their place is on the basketball floor and football field." said Floyd with enthusiasm. "Did you watch that Leroy Hemmings on TV. Man, that guy is good."

Flint joined in. "I think he can leap from the foul line all the way to the basket."

"He floats through the air." added Floyd. He was about to say something else when Earl said, "I would like to see him floating down the Kanawha River, face down."

Earl was trying to make a joke. Nobody laughed. He realized that the seriousness of the meeting was starting to deteriorate and wanted to get it back on its track. "I guess feeling the boobs through layers of clothing was like washing your feet with boots on." He smiled expectantly.

Nobody laughed although Flint had a wide smile on his face. He was trying to understand the connection that Earl was trying to make. Earl thought the smile was for his attempted humor.

Earl remarked that he would also be in the stands on St. Patrick's Day and maybe even have his family with him. He emphasized that Mavis definitely would be considered a hero in many areas. He reached into his upper suit inner pocket and took out a small parcel. "Here's ten thousand dollars to seal the deal." Mavis took the parcel and put it in her purse.

On the way back to her house Flint said that they were being followed by Floyd Maynard. He knew it was Floyd because when they pulled into the parking lot at the restaurant and Floyd pulled in near to them he noticed that one of Floyd's headlights was different colored than the other. One was bluish and the other was orangish. He must have put in a new headlight bulb that didn't match.

"Why would Floyd follow us Flint?"

"I don't know. Maybe to see if we pull off somewhere and have sex in the truck, then he could report back to Earl. Maybe, he just happens to be going in our direction. But he is back there."

"Speaking of sex Flint, I miss it with you. Maybe, we should stop somewhere and give Floyd a thrill. No, I guess that part of our relationship is over."

18. The Double Date, February 17

Larry had called Flint on Wednesday and asked if he could stay at his house for a couple of days. The rehabilitation van could drop him off after the Thursday session and Flint wouldn't have to bother himself. Mavis promised to get him a date for Saturday night so he

129

would be double dating with her and Charlie.

Flint readily agreed and said the den room was still in shape to house visitors. "Just walk in whenever you get here. I never lock the door. That makes it convenient for Marjorie who often can't find her keys in the jungle she calls a purse."

"I hope Marjorie doesn't mind my foisting myself on yunz guys."

"No, actually, she will be glad to have you here. She likes you and often asks about you."

"I like her too. Too bad you are in such an antagonistic relationship. Maybe, I better just keep my mouth shut on that subject."

"Well, for your information the antagonism has subsided and we are living in what might be called a cooperative state of coexistence." Larry said he was glad to hear it. He didn't say it, but he hoped to get another look at that attractive body of Marjorie and this time maybe exchange fluids.

It was Saturday night and the double date was the feature of the evening. Charlie had borrowed the big SUV from fellow officer Brenda Morgan in order to accommodate Larry and his stiff leg. Mavis had contacted Jane Rendell who agreed to be the date for Larry, the marine sergeant. She was looking forward to the date even though she and Larry had not yet met. Marjorie had hinted that if Larry didn't go out, neither would she and they could watch television together. Larry thanked her for the invitation but assured Marjorie he looked forward to his date with Jane Rendell and wondered what she looked like. Marjorie said she was familiar with the family, but Jane was a little girl when she last saw her about six years ago. "Sort of dumpy and plain faced."

130

Flint was already on his way to Grafton. Marjorie went up to her room and Larry could hear her talking loudly on her cell phone. He couldn't make out what she was saying, but when she came down she said words to the effect she had a date for the evening. Her date would be around to pick her up in about an hour. "Would Larry like to meet him?" "Yes, but I got to get over to Mavis and Charlie as soon as possible."

Larry decided to walk the hundred yards to the house of Mavis. He was now able to navigate slowly without the crutches, but used them on extended walks. He worried that the snow would be slippery and the crutch tips might go out from under him. He didn't think a slip and fall on the snow would injure him. His knee was well protected with the plastic cast on it.

When Larry arrived at the Kramer house he noticed the large van in the driveway and assumed Charlie had borrowed it since he knew Charlie had a small vehicle. He whistled a tune as he went up to the porch and banged one of the crutches on the porch floor boards in order to alert Mavis to his approach. Mavis heard the banging and opened the door before Larry got to it. "Larry, you wore your uniform, great. That will get us a seat up front, wherever we are going. Charlie hasn't announced our destination yet."

"I wore the uniform because my civilian wardrobe is limited. The uniform is the only thing I have resembling evening clothes."

Larry entered the kitchen which was off the porch. He put his crutches in the corner beside the refrigerator and walked over stiff legged to a chair at the table where Charlie was sitting.

Mavis seemed ecstatic. "Jane hasn't arrived yet. She will have to park out in the street. She will be staying with me overnight, so we won't have any hassle about time."

131

Jane Rendell arrived in a few minutes. Mavis watched her moving her car into a parking position. The car door opened and a strong legged young woman boldly walked up to the house. She was wearing a knee length black coat and no hat. Mavis opened the door and Jane walked in, looked at the two men rising from their chairs at the table. She wiggled her hips and said, "Ta ta." Everyone chuckled.

Mavis helped Jane take off her coat and introduced her to Charlie and "your date for the evening, Larry Reynolds." Jane walked over and shook hands with both of them. She put her face in front of Larry's.

Jane stood about five feet four in a one piece light blue dress with a darker belt around it. She had an ample bosom and her exposed flesh appeared to be smooth and taut. Her face was roundish and the bangs of her dark brown hair hung almost down to her eyebrows. When Mavis complimented her on the dress, Jane turned around and both men had a view of her rear pushing the dress out at a very pleasing angle. Charlie looked at Larry and nodded. Larry smiled back at him.

Drinks were offered by Mavis and everyone agreed to a small glass of wine. The four of them sat at the table. Jane looked at Larry, "And how is it in the marines?"

"Very fine, thank you. I must say, I was expecting to accept some dumpy hillbilly as my date, but you are gorgeous. Are you sure you want to be seen with me?"

"Flattery will get you everywhere Larry. You are gorgeous too and I am very impressed and I hope to be able to thank Mavis for arranging this meeting. I haven't dated much lately."

"Why not? " inquired Mavis. "I'm sure you have plenty of offers."

132

"Probably my disagreeable disposition. There's nobody around here that appeals to me, not even at the university." Mavis explained that she had known Jane since high school and they had become acquainted again at Clarksburg University.

"Well Charlie, where are we headed?" Mavis put the question to him.

"I thought we might go to the Magic Twanger in Fairmont. We had such a good time the last time we were there and I hoped to recapture those moments. Larry can't dance, of course, but he can listen to the music."

"And look in the faces of two beautiful women." added Larry. Both women smiled. And they were beautiful. So were the guys.

They began getting dressed to go out to the car. Jane spoke up. "My house is on the way to Fairmont if you go by Route 50. I would like to stop there and show off Larry, if you guys don't mind. I'll make some excuse like I forgot something and then my mom will say, why don't you bring your friends in so we can see them and voila, I show off Larry in his uniform." She turned to Mavis as Charlie was helping her with her coat. "I'll show off you guys too."

The back seat was accommodating with adequate floor space. Larry sat on the right, passenger side, and stretched out his leg. Jane scooted over into Larry since there was limited access. Larry didn't mind that at all, although the bulky coats made him wish it was summer. The subtle perfume of Jane had a hypnotic effect on Larry. He breathed it in with a sigh. He put his nose into her hair.

And they stopped at the Rendell home and everyone got to meet mum and dad Rendell. It was a happy introduction and everyone seemed pleased. Larry had to explain his leg that was wrapped and bulging beneath his pant leg. He lifted it up to show them the brace. He said he also had a scar on his torso and upper leg, but he didn't want to undress. They would just have to take his word for it."

Mum Rendell insisted that they pose for pictures. She arranged them in different poses, in pairs and singles. She seemed to be flitting in mid-air as she went from one side of her subjects to the other.

Dad Rendell looked closely at the ribbons on Larry's chest. There were eight of them lined up in two rows. One of them was purple. He said he didn't need an explanation for them. Larry said most of them were for drinking Middle East wine. You had to be courageous to do that."

The Magic Twanger was in full swing when the foursome arrived. Charlie had to park in the back lot. This meant that Larry would have to use his crutches.

When they arrived inside, the hostess obviously noticed Larry on crutches as well as his uniform. She told them to wait a moment while she got them a nice table. Indeed it was a nice table quite close to the bandstand. The hostess had asked the occupants to move in order to accommodate Larry and his party. Many eyes followed Larry as he moved on his crutches to the seating.

The band was again Leonard, Bubba, and whoever the other guy was. Mavis was hoping Leonard would recognize them and come over and say a few words to them. She would not be disappointed. Once he spotted Mavis and Charlie he went to the microphone. "A very slow dreamy number folks, in honor of my friends Mavis and Charlie."

Again his silver voice sang, "Oh my love, my darling, I hunger for your touch." Mavis had a chill run up and down her spine. She began to quiver. Tears welled in her eyes. "We better dance Charlie, I think I'm coming apart." They rose and hugged each other,

134

moving slowly on the crowded dance floor, bumping into other couples.

At intermission Leonard came over to their table. Mavis rose and gave him a hug. Charlie shook his hand and introduced him to Larry and Jane. Leonard said he was in the army for five years. He had a lot of friends in the military. Charlie bought Leonard a drink and asked him if he could sit with them a while. Leonard said he had a lot of preparation to do and couldn't stay. He said that after word got around that they played some slow dance music the place was jammed and he made an agreement with the management for bonuses if the take at the door exceeded eighty people. Then, he went back to arranging things on the stage.

After the trio played their now famous introduction Leonard went to the mike. "Ladies and gentlemen I would like to inform you we have a real United States Marine hero in our midst. Remember the attack on the American Embassy in Iraq where two American servicemen were killed. Well we have here one of the survivors of that attack, Sergeant Larry, a native West Virginian. Would you stand up Larry." A spotlight shone on Larry. He was embarrassed but he did stand to thunderous applause.

There was no need to buy drinks for the evening because people kept telling the waitress to give them the bill for whatever the foursome was drinking or eating. The foursome had to be careful not to overdo it. One could easily get blasted on free drinks.

Charlie danced with Jane as well as Mavis. When Charlie was dancing with Jane, Mavis and Larry would get their heads together and discuss Flint, whom Larry called George, Larry's mother and the situation with Marjorie. Larry told Mavis that he liked Marjorie very much and it was unfortunate that she seemed to be neurotic and subjected to wide mood swings. Mavis said words to the effect that Marjorie must have had something going for her to land a fabulous guy like Flint. She had to explain that everyone in the patches called him Flint, rather than George.

When the evening was almost over, two drunken male

customers came over to the table. They were both husky men wearing college sweaters, WVU and Mountaineers. The man with the WVU sweater said. "Tough marine huh. You don't look so tough to me." The band played on.

The Mountaineer sweater said, "Come on Alex, don't start any trouble."

Alex pushed him away. "Don't tell me what to do Eli. I want to see just how tough a marine can be."

Charlie, Mavis, and Jane looked around to see if anyone was watching and if the waitress would get someone to come to the rescue and get them out of this tight situation. Larry didn't take his eyes off of Alex. The music drowned everything out. It seemed particularly loud in this crises.

Mavis stood up and said, "This man is a marine and this man is a policeman, so I would advise you to move on before you get arrested."

"Or before you end up in the hospital," added Larry.

"Stand up and say that. I've punched up on many a marine." said Alex. Eli was trying to hustle him away. The music blared on. Leonard could see the situation from his spot on the bandstand. He was considering his options. Couples were shaking and twisting to the loud music. The band couldn't stop now.

Larry stood up. Charlie rose. Larry pushed him back into his seat. Alex moved forward. A waitress was moving rapidly toward them accompanied by a husky fellow who was apparently the bouncer.

Larry moved his left hand quickly into the air and snapped his fingers. Alex looked up and Larry shot a fist into the Adam's apple of Alex who collapsed on the floor gasping. Larry sat down. Jane blurted, "Oh my God, I hope you didn't kill him."

"No he'll survive but it will take a while."

The band became a two piece band as Leonard came over. "Need any help?"

Charlie assured him everything was under control. Alex was still on the floor holding his throat. The bouncer told Eli to give him a hand. They picked Alex up and between them moved him to the closest exit. The bouncer said, "We better get an ambulance."

It was impossible to get back on track. Anyway, it was near midnight and West Virginia law prohibited alcoholic sales after midnight and the band would stop playing so there was no need to tarry.

The foursome were on their feet. Larry took to his crutches as Charlie stayed near him in case the crutches should slip. Several people said, "Good job Larry" as they moved through the tables. One said "God Bless you Soldier boy."

Once in the car Larry took some deep breaths and let out some furtive gasps. Jane asked him if he was alright and he assured her he was. She put her arms around him and kissed him. Charlie laughed, "And to think this evening is just beginning."

On the way back Larry leaned against the door which he made certain was locked, stretched his leg toward the opposite door. Jane took off her shoes and curled up on the seat and leaned into him. She opened her coat, took one of Larry's hands and put it on her breast, then laid back into him. They rode back with Larry feeling both breasts and constantly kissing Jane around the neck and cheeks as well as on the lips. Mavis would turn occasionally and look at them.

When they were safely back in Kramer Manor, that's what Charlie called the home of Mavis, they sat at the kitchen table and had coffee and snacks which Mavis had prepared in advance. They washed the coffee taste away with white wine that Charlie had brought for the occasion. They moved to the living room. Charlie sat on the big easy chair and Mavis sat on his lap and nuzzled him. Jane and Larry with his outstretched leg sat on the sofa. He started nuzzling Jane.

After about ten minutes of nuzzling Mavis said she and Charlie were going into the bedroom and they might not ever come out except to use the bathroom, if that was alright with Jane and Larry who readily agreed.

As soon as Mavis and Charlie disappeared Larry began kissing Jane in earnest. He had been feeling her breasts all the way back from the Magic Twanger and now he reached for her crotch.

Jane extracted the big hard penis that was protruding underneath the marine pants. Then she slid off her panties and tried to mount it, but it was not a comfortable thing to do. She seemed defeated. "I can't get comfortable. Are you sure you can't bend your leg." Larry assured her he couldn't. They could do it sideways, but the sofa would not accommodate them. Using the floor seemed demeaning.

"I know," said Jane. She got up and went to the big chair and bent over. "Put it in right now." Larry moved rapidly, pulled the dress up over her waist, and within a matter of seconds he was in. He moved rapidly until he unloaded into her. Jane straightened up. Larry sat on the chair with his leg stretched out and Jane sat on his lap. They continued with "after play."

Jane said it was great but she would have liked to kiss Larry on the lips while they were in the act. Larry said he would have liked that also.

The evening wore on. Mavis and Charlie exited the bedroom a couple of times and tried not to look at the sofa. Both Jane and Larry appeared to be asleep, but they weren't. They were recharging their batteries.

Larry went to the bathroom and said he would wash up a

little. When he came back, Jane rose from the sofa and said she was going into the bathroom to prepare herself for the next session. Larry said he couldn't wait.

When Jane came out Larry was on his feet without pants and shorts. His leg cast was visible as was his erection. Jane moved over to him. "Where do we go from here Larry?"

"Into the kitchen my love."

"The kitchen."

There was a sturdy work table next to the sink. It was the perfect height for Larry who had cleared it off. He had set a clean towel on it and lifted Jane onto the table. She said, "Let me down." Larry lifted her from the table. She pulled her dress up around her waist and held it up. "Now put me back up there."

It was only a matter of seconds until Larry was in and moving vigorously. They exchanged a profusion of kisses and once again there was a mutually satisfying climax.

Everyone finally did get a little sleep. Larry was on the sofa and Jane was sleeping in the chair. Larry woke and looked at his wrist watch. It was quarter to seven and the sun was not up yet. He had medications to take and they were at Flint's house. He was already dressed and all he had to do was put on his shoes, get his coat and crutches and be on his way.

Once Larry stepped on the kitchen linoleum it made a loud crinkly sound and everyone was awake and moved to the kitchen. They were all bleary eyed. Mavis asked, "What's up?" Larry said he had to take some anti-infection pills and he didn't bring them with him. There was some problem developed where the new kneecap was installed. He did not want to put off the dosage. "As much as I hate to leave, I have to do it. I was awakened by some noise that sounded like a distant gunshot and so I thought I might as well get up." As he spoke there was a sharp bang outside.

Jane looked startled. "What was that? Sounded like a gunshot."

"Small caliber," said Charlie, "probably a twenty two. Someone must have shot a raccoon raiding the garbage."

Mavis was making coffee. "Those damn raccoons have really been active around here lately. They even lifted off my trash can lid and when I went out Thursday evening to put the trash in I scared two of them away. When I got to the can there was one inside, can you believe it?"

"The joys of rural living," said Charlie with a laugh. "It's still dark outside. They could have waited until everyone was up and around."

Jane offered her opinion. "The raccoons don't reckon time like we do."

Time was passing quickly. The conversation was light with laughter. They were all sipping coffee when there was another shot

Larry looked at Charlie. "That was not a 22 rifle or handgun. It was a 9 millimeter handgun, like a Beretta. A lot closer than the previous shot."

They all looked at Larry. He explained. "I have had a lot of training with military weapons fired at close and great distances. That was probably a 9 millimeter handgun. The first one that I heard was a twenty two. The shots came from two different areas and were from different caliber guns." No one challenged him. They went on sipping coffee and eating buttered toast with apricot jam on it.

Larry was dressed and ready to leave. Charlie offered to drive him the hundred yards to the home of Flint, but he declined. He pulled a cell phone from his coat pocket and asked each of them for their phone number. He installed the numbers and went to the door, followed by Jane. Mavis and Charlie moved discreetly to the living room.

Larry kissed Jane on the lips. Jane said, "Please, please, don't let this be goodbye."

"No Jane, you will have me in your life as long as you want me to be there."

Jane looked into his eyes. "That long, huh. That might be forever Larry."

"Then Forever it will be." He wrapped his arms around her.

They kissed again and Larry went out into the cold air.

Daylight was beginning to appear. The sky was clear. Planet Venus was on the low horizon. The sun would be up in a few minutes. Larry moved his crutches along the pathway down to the road. He walked along it slowly and soon he had made the hundred yards to Flint's place. Marjorie's car was in the parking lot.

Larry went past the car and started up the walk that led to the house. There was a slumped body on the walkway. He hurried to it. It was Marjorie, face down. He turned her over and looked at her face. Her eyes were wide open as were the pupils in them. He had seen that look many times. He whispered her name. He felt her neck. There was no pulse. What to do.

He took out his cell phone and dialed Mavis. She answered. "Is Charlie still there?" "Of course he is Larry what's up?"

"Tell Charlie to get over here. I just found Marjorie in the yard. She's dead."

19. Alibi

Charlie didn't arrive alone. Jane and Mavis were with him. They rushed to Larry, who was supported by crutches, standing over the body.

"Are you sure she's dead?"

"Yes, I'm sure of it, and I see the cause of death."

"What."

"See that hole in the front of the coat. That's a bullet hole." He put his finger into the small hole and lifted the coat slightly. There was blood on his finger when he extracted it from the hole. "Those shots we heard. Someone shot Marjorie. There were two different gun shots. Must have been the last one. When did we hear it"

Charlie looked at his watch. "maybe seven thirty, fifteen minutes ago." He unbuttoned Marjorie's coat. Indeed, her tan sweater had a big splash of blood. Charlie put two fingers onto the splotch of blood. It was still warm and so was the body of Marjorie.

Charlie got out his cell phone. He would call the sheriff at Clarksburg who would bring along a forensic team, if he could find them on a Sunday morning. Larry said he was going into the house and perhaps they should all go in while they waited for the sheriff to arrive. Charlie waved his hand toward the house. "You go ahead. I'll stay with the body. I see a couple of neighbors. They will all soon be over here."

The three entered the house and did not remove their coats. Larry had been trained to keep cool under stress and he used that skill to great advantage. Larry said he had a phone call to make. He didn't mind if the women heard it. He dialed and there was an immediate answer.

"Mum, it's Larry. Is George still there?"

"No, that's why I'm up. He left about an hour ago, maybe an hour and a half. What's up?"

"We just found his wife Marjorie in the yard. She was shot and killed. It's very important that you write down the time that George left your house so that you will have it documented, since the police will want that information."

"Oh my, oh my. Yes, let me see. It was around ten to seven."

"Okay mom, write that down and put it where you can find it again. Write Six, fifty. Okay."

It wasn't long until Flint was pulling into the driveway. Charlie looked at his watch and noted the time. 8:27. Flint saw Charlie and the body of Marjorie. He moved quickly to them. Charlie gave him a quick rundown on the events and told Flint he had called the sheriff who was on his way. "Who would want to harm Marjorie?" asked Flint out loud, but was asking himself.

"We hope to find that out." said Charlie. "The spouse is always suspect, so you should get your alibi together."

"I don't need an alibi, but I have one. When was she discovered?"

"Actually, just a few minutes ago. Larry found her when he left Mavis and me and he called me. Larry, Mavis, and Jane are in your house."

There was no need for Flint to inquire about the identity of Jane. He knew her from the birthday party and that Mavis was getting a date for Larry and he figured it might be the young woman named Jane. He entered the house to find all eyes on him. Mavis went over to him and hugged him. He was stiff and his body felt like a stuffed duffel bag to Mavis.

Flint went to the cupboard above the stove and took out a bottle of whiskey, got a glass from the same shelf and went over to the table. He was about to pour himself a drink when Mavis put her hand on his hand and said she wished he wouldn't drink under the circumstances. He agreed and asked her if she would make some coffee while they waited for the sheriff. Mavis kissed him on the cheek and went to look for the coffee.

The Scene

Two neighborhood women and a man arrived at the scene. A situation Charlie had anticipated. They stood at the parking area. Charlie went over to them. He flashed his wallet badge and asked them to stay in the parking area and to hold anyone else there.

There was no need to flash his badge since everyone in the neighborhood knew what Charlie looked like as well as his occupation. They were a close knit community. Maybe, too close knit.

Charlie figured there was no need to keep it from them. He said that Mrs. Haloway had been shot. One of the women said she had heard a shot about an hour ago and heard a car leaving a few minutes after the shot was fired. She didn't think anything of it. Charlie said he was expecting the sheriff at any moment and repeated for them to keep anyone else who arrived at the parking area.

The sheriff did not arrive at any moment. It seemed like time was stretching to eternity. Charlie surveyed the situation. Marjorie was about eight feet from the porch. The assailant must have been hiding on the porch waiting for her. Charlie went up on the porch and went to the side. There were footprints off to the side as if the assailant had entered the porch from that area and retreated there. He went to the front door, opened it and asked Larry to step out onto the porch.

144

Larry hobbled to the door that Charlie held open and moved out onto the porch. Charlie asked him if he noticed any footprints between Marjorie and the porch when he arrived on the scene. Larry said he hadn't thought about it, but when they arrived and were asked to go inside, he didn't remember seeing any footprints, but he couldn't be sure. If there were no footprints between Marjorie and the porch, then the assailant must have been on the porch when he shot Marjorie.

Charlie opened the door and Larry went back inside. He stood on the porch surveying the scene. A few minutes later Mavis poked her head out the door. "There were no footprints between the body and the porch. We made footprints when we came into the house." Charlie thanked her and told them to get together and remember the time they all heard the shots and to write down that Larry said they came from a nine millimeter handgun and a 22 rifle or handgun. The alleged 22 was the first shot heard.

Charlie waited in the snow. Larry told him the body was face down in the snow facing the porch when he found it. He had turned the upper part over to check for signs of life. His military knowledge and experience indicted to him that she was dead. The body was still warm under the winter coat when he, Charlie, had arrived on the scene. He still had dried blood on his fingers from when he opened the coat.

The sheriff and a deputy finally arrived. They were followed by a panel truck with the words Clarksburg Fire Department across its side. Two men were in the panel truck parked in the street. They got out, went to the back of the vehicle, extracted saw horses and put them up to block part of the road, then went back to sit in the truck.

Charlie introduced himself. The sheriff said he was Ronald Gorman and his deputy was Harry Lynch. They would do the necessary preliminaries and maybe turn the case over to the state police since they had more expertise in these matters. The body would go to the morgue and the coroner would render a verdict. Since Charlie and his friends had heard the shot, there was no need for the coroner to worry about determining the time and cause of death, "but he will be at the morgue when I call him and tell him we're comin in." Charlie said there were two shots fired at different times this morning, "may have been three. I'm sure the neighbors will be telling us the exact number of shots and the approximate times of each."

Sheriff Gorman waved to the men in the ambulance. They came to him and he said, "Harry got the photos, you can take her away. I'll be here a few minutes and meet you at the morgue. Don't unload until I get there."

One of the men went to the ambulance and came back with a stretcher. They had her body on the stretcher face up when Flint came out of the house and walked over to them. He looked down at her face that was now almost as white as the snow surrounding them. No lipstick, Eyes now closed. A look of complete serenity. He looked at one of the men standing at one end of the stretcher. "It's okay. Go ahead and do your duty." They picked up the stretcher and headed for the ambulance.

Flint looked at the sheriff. You probably need a place to sit down and write. You can come into my house and use my table. Sheriff Gorman told Deputy Lynch to interview the spectators. He would go into the house and make notes. When he was through with the neighbors Deputy Lynch should photograph more of the scene. The sun was out and the snow was starting to melt.

When they stepped onto the porch. Charlie said the footprints on the side were still pretty good. Gorman immediately summoned his deputy to photograph them. The deputy took a six inch ruler from his pocket and put it beside one of the prints, took photos of left and right and then went back to the neighbors.

Gorman said the boot print was familiar. He put his foot beside one and made a print. "I thought so, Woodland, sold by Calebos, and probably many others. By the way Mr. Haloway, would you make a footprint for us while we are here."

Flint stepped off the low porch and put his print beside one in the snow. His boot made several horizontal stripes in the snow. The Woodland footprint was in a criss-cross pattern. Flint's print was at least an inch larger than the suspect print. Sheriff Gorman noted that and also noted that his own print was about the same size as Flints.

"As snow melts, prints begin to enlarge. This guy had small feet."

"Or woman," added Charlie. "Or woman," echoed Sheriff Gorman.

Charlie told Mavis she and Jane should go back to her house. Since Larry had found the body he should remain and, of course, Flint should be here, after all, it is his house and it was his wife.

Marital situation. Not friendly. Any idea where the victim had been. No idea. Who were the victim's friends, other than neighbors? None known, but they did exist. Flint would look for evidence of them. He never went into Marjorie's room, but he would do so. Why not do it now with witnesses? Why not?

Flint headed for the stairs with the sheriff following him. Charlie stayed behind. The sheriff turned and waved him to accompany them.

Marjorie's room was well kept and everything was in a normal place. There was no second bath or shower upstairs but there was a sink and toilet in a small powder room. Towels hung neatly on a towel rack.

"You go ahead and open drawers Mr. Haloway and we will peek in them with you."

Flint went to the dresser. There were bottles of lotions and potions, some postage stamps and paper clips in a small dish, a comb, a finger nail file and a slip of folded paper.

147

Flint unfolded the paper. On it was written - **Floyd Harper, February 17.** "Today, is February 18, so she wrote this yesterday.

She must have had a meeting with this Floyd Harper yesterday." Flint handed the note to Sheriff Gorman who put it in his shirt pocket. He didn't know any Floyd Harper. Neither did Flint.

Flint opened the left top drawer which contained cosmetics, several tweezers, small scissors, a hair brush and comb. The right top drawer contained similar items, but also a lot of crumbled up pieces of paper. When Flint unfolded one of them it said - **E. A. Feb 14.** Flint realized it stood for Elmer Atkins, but he didn't mention that to the sheriff. Besides, that date was Valentine's Day and had no relevance to today's date.

Charlie said he knew what these meant. When he dated his girl friend in college she would always leave a note saying where she was going and with whom. That way, if something happened to her, there would be evidence. He chuckled, "I said there was no need to leave a note when you were going out with me. She said the hell there wasn't." They agreed, that was what Marjorie had intended.

Floyd Harper must be local and probably not hard to find."

"Except, that might not be his real name." said Flint. "Lots of guys never gave a girlfriend a real name, especially a casual girlfriend."

In the last drawer of the chest of drawers there was an envelope addressed to George Haloway, "For his eyes only."

Sheriff Gorman said it was a personal document and Flint could read it without divulging the contents to him or anyone else. If there was something relevant, then he would expect Flint to consult with him. Flint put the envelope in his back pocket that housed his wallet.

The search of Marjorie's room was finished and the three investigators went back downstairs where they found Larry with his head in his arms at the kitchen table. He looked up and it was obvious he had been crying. Tear tracks stained his face. They all looked at him. He blurted, "I really liked that lady."

Flint told Sheriff Gorman that he was in Grafton Saturday night and he had witnesses to that effect. He left Grafton and the Reynolds home around seven a.m. stopped to get gasoline at the Sheetz at the big crossroads, bought a cup of coffee and a doughnut at the Subway inside, finished that and drove straight home. Sheriff Gorman told him to get the times down and to come into his office tomorrow after work and make a notarized statement. Flint said he now had a burial to arrange and would take off work tomorrow and be in around one o'clock. Gorman said that would be fine. The fact that Flint calmly mentioned the burial in this hectic situation was something the sheriff would mull over.

Charlie said that if Larry wanted to go back home to Grafton, he would drive him there in the van. He was sure that Mavis and Jane would go along, although Mavis was supposed to pick up Chloe around noon. He looked at his watch. "My God, it is already past noon."

Larry said that Jane had her own car and probably already headed home. Charlie said that wouldn't change anything. As soon as things were settled here he would drive Larry back to Grafton. The van belonged to his fellow officer Brenda Morgan and he would return it to her sometime in the evening. Larry said he only had a small suitcase, the crutches, and they could leave immediately if the Sheriff didn't have any objections. The Sheriff said he would make arrangements to send someone over to Grafton and get a statement from Larry. Then he added, "and your mother." Michelle had a regular job and the sheriff would take that into consideration.

149

The sheriff joined his deputy and they drove off together. Charlie arrived at the house and Larry used his crutches to get to the van.

Before leaving Larry hugged Flint and said, "Keep the faith, George. It will take a while to get used to it. You didn't have her here for more than five years and she was only here a short time. Consider it an apparition that never really happened." This was similar to the way he consoled his fellow marines when one of their members was lost. He went to the van, got in the back seat and Charlie drove away.

Flint went into the house and poured himself a half glass of whiskey. He removed the envelope addressed to him from his back pocket and slit it with his pocket knife. There was a folded note inside. It read. - *My dearest George, and you are my dearest, and despite the past I know I am yours. Since you are reading this I know that something terrible has happened to me because you are honorable and would not go through my things. Do not feel bad for me or for yourself, because, despite our affection, we could never have worked it out. The money I have, was obtained from gambling in Florida. I had inside information there. You will find a small bank book in my purse and if my purse is not around then go to the Mountain Folks Bank in Parkersburg where you are listed as my next of kin and they will accommodate you. Also, there is some stacks of money on the upper shelf of the clothes closet. Have a happy life. Love Marjorie.*

Flint put his head in his arms and sobbed uncontrollable. He finally got his composure, rose and went to look out the window on the door. Two men in police uniforms were moving about the yard. People were standing in his parking lot looking at the walkway and toward his house. It would be a while before the house would no longer be a tourist attraction.

20. The Statement

Monday one o'clock. Sheriff Ronald Gorman informed Flint that this was not a formal interrogation but just a friendly conversation. If he felt there was a need for formality he would then arrange a meeting under different circumstances.

He asked Flint about Saturday night and Sunday morning.

"We went to the Grafton Inn and listened to music. Lot of our friends were there. Then we went home, had a serious discussion about our lives, sat around a while and then went to bed. I woke up around six and couldn't get back to sleep. Michelle was awake also. So we got up, had breakfast and I said I may as well be on my way. For one thing I was anxious about Larry and his leg infection was kicking up. I thought I might be needed at home."

"What time did you actually leave the house in Grafton?"

"I'm certain it was before seven because I had Ray Pflipps program on the radio and it was just starting after I was on the way out of the city."

In response to other questions Flint stated that he did not own a handgun. He had three long guns, a twelve gauge shotgun for rabbits, a 22 Hornet for squirrel, turkey and varmints, and a thirty thirty for deer.

Monday, at two o'clock, Flint gave his statement to the stenographer who let him read it and then sign it. "*I spent Saturday Evening, January 17 at the home of Mrs. Michelle Reynolds in Grafton. I left her premises slightly before seven a.m. Then drove back to my home in the Buckeye patch. On the way, I stopped at the Sheetz Gas Station at the crossroads of I 79 and U.S. Route 50 where I tanked up with gasoline and had a cup of coffee and a doughnut which I consumed on the premises. Then I drove back to my home in Buckeye, arriving around twenty minutes after eight where I was informed by Officer Charles Fitch that my wife had been shot sometime during the evening. I offer my credit card gasoline receipt as evidence for what I have stated. I paid for the coffee and*

151

doughnut with cash. "

Flint handed the gasoline receipt to the stenographer expecting her to staple it to the statement. She handed it to Sheriff Gorman who whistled, "Fifty four bucks for gasoline, you must have been running on fumes."

"No, I had a half a tank and the fill up cost around thirty two dollars."

"It says fifty four bucks here." He held it toward Flint. "Check it out."

Flint looked at the receipt. "This isn't my receipt."

Sheriff Gorman had a look of seriousness. Flint said the only thing he could think of at this time was he took the receipt out of the machine and it must have been for the vehicle that filled up before he got there. His receipt probably popped up after he left the pumps. The next person was hopefully more alert and probably threw it in the trash can next to the pumps.

"Maybe, if you go over there right now and check out the trash can you can find it. You say, around thirty dollars. Anyway, it would have the last four digits of your credit card number on it as well as yesterday's date. We can get that information from your credit card company, but it would save us a lot of hassle if the receipt could be found."

Flint said he would leave immediately. Sheriff Gorman told Deputy Harry Lynch to go with him. They could kill two birds with one stone, search for the receipt in the trash can next to the pump and Deputy Lynch could validate Flint's appearance in the snack shop where he had the doughnut.

Lynch offered to drive the squad car. Flint thought that would attract too much attention. They would take Flint's pick-up. The crossroads was only about ten miles from Clarksburg.

Flint took the lid off the trash can that served Pump 4 and looked inside. There wasn't much in it, but obviously it had not been emptied. There were many receipts in the can. Didn't anyone keep their gasoline receipts?

Flint retrieved as many receipts as possible from the top of the trash and looked at the amount of the purchase and if the purchase was around thirty dollars he would look at the four digits printed on the receipt. This was the last four digits on his credit card. He didn't find his receipt.

There was nothing to do but to take out the plastic liner and go through the entire lot of trash. He moved to the trash can at the next pump. Trash Can for Number Five.

Slowly he removed each piece of trash from can number four and deposited it in can number five. A banana peel, several empty soft drink cans, two envelopes with letters in them, much more. Deputy Lynch suggested they quit this foolishness and let the sheriff contact the credit card company.

Flint hit pay dirt. He found the receipt. February 18, Time 7:18 a.m. Thirty two dollars and fifty six cents, and the credit card number 7765.

Flint smiled at Deputy Lynch. "Let's go inside and I'll buy you a coffee and a doughnut."

"No sir, I will buy you a coffee and a doughnut. You go to the rest room and wash your hands. I'll take that receipt." Flint handed it to him.

Deputy Lynch was sitting on a stool at the snack bar. Flint took the seat beside him. There were two cups of coffee and two doughnuts in front of him. He pushed a set over to Flint. "Is that the waitress who waited on you?" Flint said it was and he would not be able to forget that face.

"Okay George, do your thing."

"Friends call me Flint."

Harry Lynch looked serious. "I like you buddy, but I am not your friend yet."

The waitress had a plastic tag on her uniform. "Louise - How May I Help You." Flint motioned for Louise to move closer. "I was in here yesterday morning, do you remember me?"

Louise looked at him. The fact that Deputy Lynch was in uniform made her a little suspicious. A lot of cops came into the place, but always with other cops and not with someone in ordinary clothes. She wasn't sure how to react. She had noticed them rooting through the trash can and tried to understand what they were doing, but couldn't think of anything except they were looking for some lost item.

"Lot of people come in here and I can't remember them all." She was obviously trying to assist Flint in his endeavor but was not sure if she was taking the right course of action.

"You will remember me because I remarked about your long stockings and you said that your legs got tired, being on your feet all day, and the tight stockings helped keep your muscles from collapsing."

Louise realized that Flint wanted verification. "Yeah, I remember. You said I had nice leg muscles and maybe you could rub them for me if the stockings didn't work out. That was a good come on. I was tempted to give you my phone number. Too bad you scooted out of here."

"Hey Louise, if you're still game, I will take that phone

number. I'll call you and we can get to know each other over the phone and if that works out we can proceed from there."

Louise said she would like that. She turned over a small order pad and wrote her number on it. "Don't keep me waiting." Flint assured her he wouldn't. He wrote his name on the back of another pad, "Flint Haloway." He didn't put a phone number beside it.

On the way back to the police station Deputy Lynch said he was amazed at how quickly Flint made contact with the waitress. He would assure Sheriff Gorman that Flint's alibi would hold up. "That Louise is pretty and has a great body on her." Flint agreed with him."But, apparently, she has weak calf muscles." They both laughed out loud.

Flint asked Deputy Harry Lynch if he was taken aback by the fact that he had hit on Louise when his wife was just murdered yesterday. "No, I'm not surprised. Sheriff Gorman told me about the slips of paper with men's names on them and the dates of the meetings. And that you had been separated a long time and she had just returned a short while ago. You are probably still in shock at her death as well as her mysterious return. It will really hit you in a day or two. Course I don't know the details."

Flint gave Deputy Lynch a quick rundown on his marriage to Marjorie. He had finished a two year degree in forestry at Mount Alto in Pennsylvania. He couldn't get a job in forestry so he took one with the gas company. He was twenty six years old when he met Marjorie. He knew she had several former boyfriends, but that didn't bother him. She was just a great person to be with. After a little more than two years of marriage, Marjorie found out she couldn't have children. She took that pretty hard. About a year after that she took off and sent a postcard from Florida. There was no more contact until she showed up in the area a couple of months ago. It was nerve wracking wondering where she was and how was she getting along. Actually, the event of her death was some sort of closure. He hoped he didn't sound like he was happy about the situation. He really did like Marjorie and hoped for the best for her.

Flint had another conversation piece for Deputy Lynch. This was the first woman he had ever hit on. He was inept at flirtation and all the women that he had intimate relations with had come on to him. He really didn't know how to come on to women. Deputy Lynch said he didn't know how to come on to women either and he admired guys that could. That's why he was impressed with Flint's aggression with Louise.

There was silence for a while and then Flint made an attempt to lighten things up. "Well, Deputy Lynch why do you keep referring to your boss as Sheriff Gorman instead of Ron or Ronald?"

"I usually refer to him as Ron, but I wanted you to be certain whom we were talking about."

"That's a pretty good job you have, second in command of a large police department."

"You don't know the set up very well. Believe it or not, there are six different positions between the Sheriff and the Deputy Sheriff. I'm just a gopher. There is an Assistant Sheriff who has a desk job with a lot of authority. She is about to retire and that is the job that I'm after. That would put me about third or fourth in command. I forget the exact order of importance. We keep getting reminders of our duties and responsibilities in the hierarchy, and I am at the bottom of it."

Flint dropped Deputy Lynch off at the station then drove home. Sheriff Gorman read the statement that Flint had signed to Deputy

Lynch. The sheriff said, "He could have come here, shot his wife, and then went back to the gas station to create an alibi."

Lynch looked at the times indicated and wrote them on a pad. "He would have had to exceed the speed limit. Maybe, we should give him a traffic ticket for speeding." The sheriff didn't laugh, but agreed that he would have had to exceed the speed limit. That was no problem in West Virginia where very few people observed the speed limit on the open road.

21. The Bank Manager

The Mountain Folks Bank in Parkersburg was open until noon on Saturdays. They opened at nine. Flint was there shortly after opening and asked if there was someone he could talk to about a confidential financial matter. The teller walked out from behind the counter and told him to follow her. She led him to a door that said Manager, poked her head in and asked if it was okay to let someone in. She got the okay, opened the door wider, and ushered Flint into the office.

A distinguished looking man in a light gray suit sat behind a desk. He had dark eyebrows and lighter colored hair with gray at the temples. He sported a thin mustache which seemed coordinated to his hairstyle. Flint looked at the name plate. Floyd Harper - Manager.

"My name is George Haloway."

"I know who you are and now you know who I am. No need for you to call Sheriff Ronald Gorman, he was here almost immediately. More competent than he looks." Harper rose and pulled a chair from the front of the desk and placed it nearer to his. "Please, have a seat and I'll tell you the story." Flint was uneasy as he took the intended seat. Floyd Harper was obviously a take charge kind of guy and was adept at telling people what to do and make them think it was their idea to do it.

"I met Marjorie when she made her bank deposits and we hit it off immediately. I am between marriages and so am free to navigate socially. We liked each other very much and even talked about getting married. She still seemed like she thought you two might get back together and so was reluctant to consider the possibility. She made no bones about having another intimate friend beside me."

"Yeah, Marjorie was never devious, always was straight forward."

"I hope you can handle this without anger or a sense of recrimination." Flint said he could.

Floyd Harper continued. "On Saturday night we went out to dinner and listened to a string quartet for about two hours. Then we went back to my place and lounged around and went to bed. There was no need to hide anything about our association. We are all adults."

"Sometimes, I don't feel like an adult."

"I'm with you on that. Anyway, we were up about five o'clock. We showered together and Marjorie said she wanted to go home. It was getting daylight and the sun was coming up and she hated sunshine. She didn't want to stay around any longer. We went to breakfast at the Perkins. Restaurant. As I told the sheriff, I paid and left a tip in cash. I don't have my times straight, but I know I dropped her off around seven. I didn't know about the death until Tuesday morning when Sheriff Gorman showed up. I seldom watch the news or read the newspaper, except the Wall Street Journal."

"I guess it wouldn't be in the Wall Street Journal." Flint smiled. Extended his hand to Harper who shook it. "No hard feelings. I appreciate you're entertaining Marjorie. God knows she must have been in some sort of turmoil. She seemed to be coming out of it and association with you must have been good therapy for her."

"I believe she was getting her life together pretty good, George. Who would want her dead? Certainly not you. Based on what she said. And, of course, not me. I did feel it necessary to tell the police about the amount of money that would be legally yours now that Marjorie is gone."

"Of course. The first suspect is always the spouse. But, I had nothing to do with it."

"I'm certain you didn't. Marjorie said more than once that you are an honorable man and anyone could trust you with his life."

Flint grimaced. "She was overstating the facts. There are some people who couldn't trust me with their life."

Floyd Harper pulled a manila folder out of this lower desk drawer. "I was waiting for your arrival, so I have this on hand. Since you have no children, you should name a beneficiary."

"I don't think I need one at this time."

"Think about it George. If someone gunned down Marjorie they might also have you in mind."

"Let me sleep on it a few days." Flint hadn't expected the large amount of money now at his disposal. "How can you put two hundred thousand in the bank without the FBI inquiring about its origin? Aren't you obligated to report large amounts of cash deposits to them?"

Floyd Harper smiled. "It's called creative bookkeeping. We can cover large cash deposits as long as we can come up with reasons for it. In this case, Marjorie had a receipt from a Rudolph Vanilla testifying to winning it at his casino. Of course, I gave his name to Sheriff Ronald Gorman.

On the way home Flint thought about the funny things Marjorie used to say. He thought about the statement on sunrise that Harper had made. He got tears in his eyes when he thought about one of Marjorie's favorite sayings, "I hope the sun doesn't come out and shit up my whole day."

Flint thought about beneficiaries. He could only think of Mavis Kramer and Michelle Reynolds. Maybe, the Salvation Army, they do a lot of good. How could a man his age not have any beneficiaries? That bothered him.

Sheriff Ronald Gorman, Deputy Harry Lynch and stenographer Marianne Schultz were at the home of Michelle Reynolds. Larry Reynolds was also there.

Larry gave his account of what transpired. He said the first shot heard was around six thirty and the second shot around seven thirty, maybe seven fifteen. It was his opinion that the first shot was by a 22 rifle or handgun and the second shot was by a higher caliber. In his opinion it was a nine millimeter handgun. Many of his comrades privately owned a nine millimeter handgun and they practiced shooting on a regular basis. He knew the exact sound it makes. Sheriff Gorman said he would accept that opinion but not consider it gospel.

The marine hero described finding the body face down, head toward the porch and turning it over slightly to see if Marjorie was still alive. She wasn't. He felt her neck for a pulse to make certain that she wasn't alive. He then called Officer Charles Fitch who was in the house he had just departed. Officer Fitch came over and took charge of the scene until Sheriff Ronald Gorman and his crew arrived.

The statement was put in formal language, typed up on a laptop computer, printed and signed by Lawrence Reynolds.

Michelle Reynolds did not seem to be nervous, but was obviously upset by the events. Everyone connected somehow to the events was upset. Sheriff Gorman tried to get her to relax.

Michelle went over the events of Friday evening even though it was not pertinent to her statement. She said that George Haloway left her home sometime before seven o'clock on Sunday morning. She knew the time because she had turned on the television shortly after he left.

Did George Haloway always leave at that early hour? No, he didn't. He woke up around five thirty and couldn't get back to sleep, so he rose, ate a quick breakfast and he left.

What was his mood? Did he seem upset about anything?

Mrs. Michelle Reynolds bit her lip. "He might have been upset."

"Could you elaborate. If you will?"

"Yes, I don't have any secrets. I told George that we were on a treadmill and there was no future in it for us. We enjoyed each other's company, but I met a man who might be in my future and if George didn't mind, I would see this other gentlemen from time to time on a personal basis. I thought we might shift our usually every Saturday visits to every other Saturday. George said that would be fine with him. He always had a lot of activities scheduled for Saturdays anyway."

"Did he mention what those activities were?"

"Oh, he said something about tending to his sheep. You know he and another fellow raise pure bred sheep that they sell for a pretty good profit. He is also some kind of officer in some kind of gun organization. He assured me he could use a Saturday night at home once in a while. He might have been saying that because he felt I wanted him to say that."

Sheriff Gorman gave an opinion. "I guess that is irrelevant." He turned to the stenographer, "Just get the time Haloway left the home of Mrs. Reynolds. That is the relevant point."

After the sheriff and his entourage departed, Michelle turned to her son. "You don't think George killed his wife, do you?"

"No, I don't. They had a good understanding relationship and were working it out. Can't think of anyone who would want to hurt Marjorie, she was a very nice lady."

Mother Reynolds noticed tears forming in her son's eyes. "Even George thought so, didn't he?" She changed the subject. "When do I get to meet this Jane that you have been raving about."

"She's coming over this Saturday. We will be going out and I hope she agrees to stay overnight with me."

"I'll be here to greet her, since George Haloway is busy. Mr. Arnold said we should cool it under the circumstances."

"I think Thomas Arnold is a good match for you, about your age and very dignified and businesslike. He is not a masculine fireball like George, but he is what I consider to be ideal in a father figure. However, I hate to think I have a mother who sleeps around."

"I don't sleep around. Any sleeping I do will be right here in my own home. Besides, with Thomas, I don't get in much sleeping."

Larry grimaced. His mother laughed, "That's a joke you know."

22
Sheriff has a Theory

Sheriff Ronald Gorman had a serious expression as they left the Reynold house. Deputy Harry Lynch pulled out onto Route 50 and headed west toward Clarksburg. Harry took his eyes off the road for a second and looked at him. "What are you thinking?"

"Just a thought we might consider possibilities. We have Larry's word for the caliber of the two guns that were heard on the fatal day. He was the only one of the four that heard the first shot. Two shots were confirmed by neighbors who didn't have a clue about calibers. One neighbor said there were three shots. Here is a possibility. Larry got up early, shot Marjorie with a nine millimeter, went back to the Kramer house and pretended he just got up. The second shot was convenient. He could identify it as a nine millimeter and no one would challenge him. Charlie Fitch was too absorbed in the party to give it much thought."

"Why would Larry want to shoot Marjorie? He handled the situation correctly by calling Charlie Fitch to the scene. He even had tears in his eyes when I saw him."

"That is something to consider. I am only conjecturing you understand. It's possible he wanted to protect his mother's interest in her boyfriend Haloway. By killing the wife, Haloway would be free to marry his mother."

Deputy Lynch thought it over. "It could be the way you described, but I doubt it."

"I doubt it too." Sheriff Gorman shook his head. "I understand there is a coffee and doughnut shop near here. Let's stop and have some refreshments. I have been timing how long it takes us to get from the Reynold's home to the coffee shop, at the legal speed limit."

"I'm going a little over the limit. West Virginian, you know."

"Oh, yes Harry. Get on the computer and find out what time sunrise occurred on February 17. Everyone keeps talking about the sun not being up yet and sun rising. We should know the exact time and give some thought to dawning and morning glow."

"Sun rose at seven fifteen exactly on February seventeen, set at six oh six. I already looked it up." Deputy Lynch paused. "What did you find out about that guy in Florida? The one who brought Marjorie north?"

"His name is Rudolph Vanilla and they had lived together for about a year. I talked to him on the phone and checked him out here and had the locals check him out down there. He drove Marjorie to Clarksburg where they stayed at the Best Western on I-79 for a week before she went home. He is connected with horse racing and casinos. Quite wealthy. He was in Florida when Marjorie was killed."

Deputy Lynch suggested that Mr. Vanilla might have been in some illegal activities and Marjorie knew about them, so he hired a hit man to come north and get Marjorie. Sheriff Gorman said that was a possibility, but the idea seemed far-fetched. Anyway, the district attorney in Florida assured me that they had thoroughly investigated the activities of Rudolph Vanilla many times and had never found anything remotely illegal about him. The guy is worth many millions. The amount of money Marjorie had in her account would be a drop in his bucket."

"How about Floyd Harper the banker?" Lynch just threw that out. "He could have shot Marjorie for some unknown personal reason and then give us the story about dropping her off and all that."

Sheriff Ronald wheezed. "Naw, Harper struck me as being a straight arrow."

164

"Rule of the jungle. Let no stone be left unturned."

They were approaching the Subway restaurant sign. "Here's another thought Harry. What if George Haloway left the Reynolds house closer to six thirty than to seven and convinced Mrs. Reynolds that it was near seven. He would have ample time to shoot his wife and high tail it back to the crossroads and get a gasoline receipt. I still have to work on that time angle and factor in sunrise."

"If Haloway needed a receipt, I think he would have made certain he kept it."

"He might have had the receipt all along and given us the phoney one to make it look like he was just stumbling along."

"Let's don't forget he said something about killing her to one of his buddies at lunch just after she got back into his house."

"That's just an expression Ron." laughed Harry. "Do you have any idea how many times I said I felt like killing you?"

Deputy Harry Lynch pulled into the parking lot at the Sheetz Subway gas station complex. "I believe Haloway's story. He seems genuinely broken up by his wife's murder. Little things, like his expressions. Some neighbors I interviewed thought they had worked out an amiable compromise on living together. Everyone I talked to said they liked her."

"Well, she's dead and it's our job to find out who did it."

March 7. Wednesday

The days moved into March and Earl Hazzard would check off each day on his calendar. He was fidgety and couldn't think about anything except the great event that would occur on St. Patrick's Day which handily came on a Saturday this year. He seemed to be able to think of nothing else.

The first March meeting of the militia was on the first Wednesday of the month. They met at their building at seven in the evening. Participants brought beer, thermoses of coffee and snacks. To almost everyone's surprise and to Earl's delight there were eighteen people in attendance.

Before the meeting, Elmer Atkins called Flint aside and offered condolences. Flint knew his offering was sincere. He liked Elmer and Alicia and their sexual activities did not discourage, but rather enhanced that opinion. Flint thanked Elmer and said he appreciated Elmer's attention to Marjorie, otherwise they might have spent a lot of evenings arguing with each other.

When Flint was through talking to Elmer, Ward Hollister. partner in sheep raising, sought him out. "A fellow from Virginia, on the other side of Bluefield came up yesterday and dropped off two ewes that he thought were ready for breeding. I can't be there for the full treatment on that quick notice. Have to go to Wheeling and give a deposition about my brother's partnership with me and my other brother. Would you be able to get over there and take charge. I don't think Miriam can handle it by herself."

Flint thought about it. "Yeah, I could do that sometime in the afternoon. I'm on gas well reading this week and sort of my own boss. Tell Miriam I'll be there shortly after noon."

"I have the two ewes in the small enclosure and the ram locked up in his usual pen. He has been butting his head at the gate, so I guess the owner was correct and the ewes were in estrus. I let him have a crack at one of them and then had a hellova time getting them back in their separate pens."

"Don't fret it. As you know, I've handled it before and know how to go about it."

166

"If everyone is done socializing I guess it's time to start the meeting." Earl's eyes were glassy, as if he had been smoking weed. However, everyone knew that he did not indulge in drugs and was very adamant about shooting drug dealers and druggies. That is, he put them in that category along with the other people he would like to shoot. It was a long list.

"I want to start off this meeting by reading you a notice I got from the National Rifle Association. I know about half of you got this notice and I bet half of that never read it. I would like to read it and we can discuss it."

Earl read slowly and with emphasis: "Dear NRA Member. Every day the national media devotes millions of dollars of free airtime to attack our constitutional right to keep and bear arms. All too often the media lets gun-hating politicians say anything they want in their drive to tear down the Second Amendment."

Earl paused and looked up, then went back to the paper. "The media lies and lets these politicians label commonly owned hunting rifles as assault weapons. They lie about crime and blame the reprehensible actions of violent criminals on our Second Amendment freedoms. They lie and give cover to U.N diplomats conspiring to ram through a global gun ban treaty and destroy your rights. They push dishonest and misleading editorials. The stories of what good people do with firearms are suppressed and never told. And slowly but surely, they're twisting a death dagger into the heart of the Second Amendment."

Floyd Maynard butted in. "They got that right."

Earl kept on reading. "I really need your help to get the truth out all across America and I'm counting on your support once again. Your one, two, or three dollar contribution to the NRA Voice of

Freedom Fund supports NRA efforts to tell the truth on TV, on the radio, in newspaper ads and on the web. In order to protect our firearm freedoms we need to fight the media lies. We can win this fight, but we need you. Signed by the NRA president."

Earl smiled as he looked up. "Any discussion."

Elmer said it was signed by the executive director and not the president. Earl followed that statement with, "there are too many chiefs and not enough Indians."

Floyd thought perhaps the Mountaineer Militia could raise money for the cause. He remembered the alleged packet of money Earl had given to Mavis. Why didn't Earl give that money to the cause? He didn't voice that opinion, but it rattled around in his head.

Jimmy Crtichlow said that "most of us are members of the NRA and our dues and other contributions should suffice." He also thought the NRA received a lot of money from gun manufacturers and the NRA never divulged the salaries of their top officials or exactly how much money was in the treasury.

Dan thought everyone should take down the address and if anyone wanted to send money to the NRA they could. Earl upstaged him by producing a pack of contribution slips with the name and address on it. He distributed a slip to each person in attendance.

Eddie warned the others to not let the letter sucker you into donations, they have tons of money and still ask for more. He was repeating what Jimmy had just stated. He would like to know the salary and the budget expenditures of the organization. He has been a member for over thirty years and has never seen a budget or what exactly they spend the money on. Other people added to Eddie's complaint about openness.

Dan said he thought when he joined this militia group they would be doing more with hunting and fishing and less with political activity. Perhaps they should invite Marcia Butler to give a little talk on her points of view concerning the environment.

Earl was almost seething at the mere mention of Marcia Butler. "If Fred Kramer had been more efficient, we wouldn't be talking about Marcia Butler. I would rather have a session with vampires than have Marcia Butler come here. They could have my blood. Marcia Butler and her cohorts are already taking our blood and money and turning it into blood money."

"Well anyway," countered Dan, "we have some good times together, but we seem to be spending too much time on politics. That's my opinion for what its worth." He was supported by comments from Coach and Alfie.

Earl assured them that events were moving rapidly and the Mountaineer Militia would soon be on the map. Coach followed that statement with, "I think maybe we should change our name to Mountain State Gun Club, or maybe Mountain State Rod and Gun Club. When Eddie suggested Mountain State Outdoor Club, Earl really became angry. "No, we agreed that the name would be Mountaineer Militia and we will stick to it as long as I am president and commander of this post."

"I don't mean this personally Earl," said Coach, "but when do we have elections. You been commander now for about ten years."

"If you read the bylaws, you can call for an election any time with the petition of three-fourths of the membership. At present we have twenty three paid dues members. Some mathematician will have to figure out what three-fourths of that is." He laughed and his laugh always sent a chill up the spine of Flint.

Floyd Maynard assured Earl that he had the support of everyone in the group and he had been an excellent leader. He was seconded by Elmer Atkins. Two or three other people made their approval known. Everyone seemed to let it go. Those who disagreed would be in action some time in the future.

169

"According to military law," said Earl with an air of authority, "some of us are due for promotions. I am now qualified for the rank of Major. Flint and Floyd qualify for Captain and Elmer for First Lieutenant." Flint raised his eyebrows at Jimmy and nodded as if to say, "how about that?"

When the meeting was over, Earl asked Flint to stay behind, he had some ideas to discuss with him. Everyone left the building. Flint asked, "What's up."

"I have the money for Mavis. It's four hundred thousand and that's it. Do you think she will accept that. You seem to be her council in this matter. It's all in fifty dollar bills."

"I'm sure she will accept that amount. She is anxious to set up a trust fund for her daughter and this will do it." Flint took the money box from Earl. He was surprised at how small it was. He estimated the measurements at four inches thick, twelve or fourteen inches square.

Earl said that they would probably have no more contact with each other until St. Patrick's Day. However, if there were any problems to contact him immediately. Flint didn't think there would be any problems.

Flint was to deliver Mavis to the militia building at eight in the morning with her costume. She would be fitted with the explosive vest and given instructions on how to detonate it. Flint felt creepy as Earl outlined the plan with serious precision. "Once fitted with the vest, she should get into her costume. Instead of getting on the band bus you will deliver her to the Oglebee Square where the festivities are to take place. The band will already be there. Once she sees the dignitaries are on the speaker stand she is to go over to that place and use the detonator. I might take my family there and watch the action. Do you have any questions?"

"No. I got it," said Flint.

Earl handed Flint a large envelope. "Here is a good photo of the Secretary of State. Mavis can study it. We don't want her making a mistake like Fred did."

23
March 8 - Thursday. The Ram Caper

It was Thursday and shortly after noon when Flint pulled into the sheep ranch. He could see the two new ewes in the small holding area separated from the flock of sheep in the pasture. The snow had melted away and the sheep in the pasture were munching on freshly uncovered vegetation as well as a pile of hay. Every sheep in the pasture was a blue-blood with a tag in its ear and certification papers locked away in Ward Hollister's house. He took in over sixty thousand dollars last year on his sheep works while his daytime job paid him not quite forty thousand. Flint's share of the partnership netted him around twenty four thousand. Ward offered to buy Flint out many times, but Flint liked the idea of owning sheep, even if it was on Ward's land and Ward and Miriam did most of the work.

There was a panel truck in the driveway and Miriam was talking to a man standing beside the driver side door. The man got in the truck and drove away.

Miriam came over to Flint's truck. She said the man in the panel truck was the owner of the ewes. He would be back at the end of the week to fetch his property and pay the stud fee. "I've got a few chores to do inside and I'll change my clothes and be out to assist you in about a half hour. Look around and size up the problem. This is gonna bring us in about five thousand dollars." She turned and headed for the house.

171

Flint knew several ways to get the heated ewes into position for the ram. He moved one ewe into the chute like pen. It was an enclosure about thirty inches wide and six feet long. The ewe would be up front facing the gate made of slats which were about a foot apart and the ram would be behind her with his back to the other gate that was made of the same slat boards about a foot apart.

The ewes were fitted with collars and Flint took the closest one from the pen and led it to the breeding chute. He put it in the chute head first and locked the gate behind her. Then he went for the ram that was scratching at the hay on the floor of his stall. He avoided the horns pointing toward him, moved around and grabbed the ram by the collar. With difficulty he led the ram to the holding chute, opened the gate and let him go in.

Within minutes the ram was up on the ewe and pumping away. Flint watched the pointed penis withdraw with much dripping. He went to a small bench where he could watch the action. He would wait an hour and change the ewes. This was a two day procedure if the ewes were still in estrus and Ward would be back to take over tomorrow. It was necessary for someone to be on hand in order not to have the ewes damaged by the ram or by some other factor unforeseen. If any ewe died while in their care it would cost them over ten thousand dollars.

Miriam came out with a thermos of coffee and handed a cup to Flint and poured him some coffee. She was dressed in form fitting jeans, a jean's jacket and wearing red boots. Flint looked at her. "Don't you look gorgeous. If I were you I wouldn't let the ram get a look at those red boots. Your ass would be in danger."

"How do you like the boots. I used to be in a troupe of folk dancers and we wore red boots as part of the act. Now I don't do folk dancing and thought I would get some use out of the boots."

"Very nice looking boots, I must say. And so is the rest of

172

your outfit."

Miriam puffed out her already puffy lips. "How's it going?"

"Go over and take a look." Flint drank from the metal cup.

Miriam went over to the breeding chute and watched the ram mount the ewe and pull back with his pointed red penis dripping. She seemed fascinated and frozen in place. Flint came over beside her.

She took her eyes off the scene momentarily and looked at Flint. "You know I have seen this action out in the field many times, but I was never up this close to it." She turned her gaze back to the slats in the chute. They stood there awhile. Flint said he would go back for more coffee. He needed to sit down.

Miriam was fixated on the pen and the scene. Flint finished his coffee and went over to her. "Any problem?"

"No, it's just that I was never this close before. I didn't realize that the ram had such big balls."

"Maybe you want to hold and feel them." said Flint with a laugh.

He was put back when Miriam said she would like to do that if it was possible. There was silence. Miriam had a look of anticipation. Okay, Flint could arrange that if she really wanted to do that.

Flint took a four foot long two by four from a stack on the floor by the wall. He went over to the chute and when the ram backed off he put the two by four through the chute and had the ram trapped with his tail to the chute back gate. He turned to Marian. "Just go back and reach through the slats and massage the balls." Marian was all smiles.

She reached through the back gate and took the testicles in her right hand and squeezed them over and over again. She moved

173

her hand forward and felt the sheath that enclosed the penis. She moved from one testicle to the other and moved them up and down. When she had enough satisfaction she moved her hand back through the slats and smelled it. "Strong odor."

"Had enough? Shall I release Cyrus." Miriam said he could. Flint pulled the two by four out of its position and Cyrus was back on top of the ewe.

Flint said he would shift ewes in about an hour. He wouldn't want Cyrus to waste his days ration on one maiden. Anyway this ritual would last at least another day. Miriam wasn't responding. She was transfixed on the red penis going in and out and dripping.

Finally, she turned to Flint. "Would you do me a favor?"

"If I can."

"This might sound crazy. I want to get on my knees and have you put it into me and make believe it's the ram behind me."

"That is crazy Miriam, but I certainly like the idea."

Flint complied with the request. It was so pleasing to Flint that it only lasted about six minutes. He tried to delay it, but lost control.

Flint sat on the bench while Miriam finished dressing. She came over to him. "That was some fantasy." Flint assured her it wasn't fantasy to him, it was real and sensational. He remarked that Ward was indeed lucky to get that kind of satisfaction with Miriam. She indicated in a way that Ward did get satisfaction, but not the kind she and Flint had enjoyed.

When Flint hinted he would enjoy an encore, Miriam said there would be none. She didn't want to ruin the enchantment of the moment. Flint thought to himself, *yes, enchantment. That's the word for it*

Miriam said she was going into the house to lie down. The event had drained her of all her strength. The emotion was overwhelming. Flint said that if Miriam wanted a repeat performance, he was willing to please her. After all, it had been about six weeks since he and Michelle last got it on. Michelle wanted to hold off until the murder of Marjorie was solved so he was cut out of sex for the time being.

Miriam patted Flint on the arm. She said that a repeat of the original performance could not possibly reach the same level of perfection. If Flint wanted more of her and she was willing, there might be another time, "but don't count on it."

24
March 9 - Friday

Flint and Mavis had an appointment with bank manager Floyd Harper for eleven o'clock. Mavis had no classes on Friday so she was free. Chloe was with Mildred. There was no danger to Chloe at this time since the betrayal she planned had not yet been effected.

Manager Harper greeted them with a warmth that was not pretentious. Flint thought how fortunate Marjorie had been to have associated with such a nice gentleman. He was certain she had enjoyed her last evening with him even though she probably wanted another crack at Larry.

Flint put the package on the desk. Manager Harper picked it up and noted the UPS shipping label was still on it. The address on the label was that of Earl Hazzard. Flint said it never occurred to him to consider the label. This could be valuable evidence. Harper didn't ask "evidence for what" but he was thinking it.

Flint took out his pocket knife and cut the top cover from the package. He cut around the label and put it in his upper shirt pocket and threw the remaining cardboard into the wastebasket at the side of the desk.

Harper pulled the contents from the open box. The money

175

was wrapped in black denim. The manager took a pair of scissors from his desk drawer and cut away the denim exposing stacks of fifty dollar bills. He asked Mavis and Flint to take a seat as he got on the inter-office phone. "Clifford, come to the office and bring the counter with you."

It was only a matter of minutes when Clifford came into the office with a machine that looked like a large duplicating machine. "This machine will count the money in a matter of minutes."

There were sixteen shrink wrapped packets. Manager Harper opened them one at a time and handed them to Clifford who fed them into the machine. Harper turned to Mavis and Flint, "These are nice crisp bills and easily handled by the machine."

It took only twenty minutes. Clifford pushed the print button and the machine popped out a long slip of paper. Manager Harper directed Clifford to put the money in the safe and he will take care of it when this meeting was concluded. Clifford put the box of money on top of the machine and wheeled it out of the room.

"Exactly four hundred thousand dollars." He looked at Mavis and Flint who were both sitting with somewhat glazed eyes. "Can you tell me the source of this money?"

"I don't know Floyd, it's kinda personal," said Flint.

Mavis had a reason. "You know about my brother who shot a lady in Charleston and was himself shot by the police."

"Yes, I'm quite familiar with the story."

"Well," said Mavis with sincerity, "people felt so sorry for me that donations started pouring in and this money was the result."

"I'll buy that and so will the IRS since they will be getting a big cut out of the donations? The IRS doesn't much care where the money came from, as long as you pay taxes on it."

Harper took a seat on his desk. "I think it would come to about ten percent. I will take five thousand dollars out of your account and pay an accountant to handle the paper work, if that's okay with you Miss Kramer."

Mavis looked at Flint who nodded. "Yeah, that would be fine. How much would that leave me?"

"Oh with various fees and such, you would probably have around three hundred and fifty thousand in your savings account. I assume you will start investing some of it and I am here to advise you on investments."

Harper had many documents for Mavis to sign. When it came to beneficiaries she listed Chloe and Mrs. Mildred Perkins to act as guardian until Chloe reached age eighteen. Harper put his notary seal on the document.

It was after one o'clock when they left the bank and entered the restaurant. Mavis said it would be her treat since she was now a wealthy woman and had around ten thousand dollars in cash at her disposal.

They again went over the plan for the St. Patrick's Day celebration. On tomorrow's Saturday date, Mavis would ask Charlie to move in with her since he was now living with his mother and was assigned to the Clarksburg state police station for a year at least.

Mavis said she was planning on doing that anyway.

On St. Patrick's Day at around six in the morning, she would say she was having stomach and chest pains and would Charlie take her to the emergency room at the hospital. If she could vomit at the hospital that would be an asset. She hoped she could manage it.

"I will take your bear costume to the meeting with Earl and

the others and after much discussion I'll suggest that since Earl is the same height as you, he should get in the costume, go to the parade and detonate the bomb."

"What if he wants to do that?"

"No way he would do that. Big talkers and macho men are all cowards at heart. That's why they talk big. He will find some excuse and that will be our reason to abandon him."

"What if he tries to get his money back or revenge?"

"Charlie will be with you at the hospital and he will be living with you, so that would be your protection. I will also be keeping an eye on Earl."

Mavis blurted out. "The police already have Earl under surveillance." She gasped, "I wasn't supposed to tell anybody that."

"You can trust me. What else do you know that you weren't supposed to tell anyone."

Mavis hesitated. "When they examined Marjorie they found the bullet in her clothing. They also found a shell casing near your porch under the snow. Charlie thinks the assailant looked for it but couldn't find it in the snow, but the forensic team did. At least they think it is the casing since casings are not commonly found in front of people's porches."

"Why are they watching Earl. So far he's clean."

Mavis went on to quote Charlie. Earl's boots were the same brand that made imprints in the snow off the porch. The police have been looking for clues that would lead them to a large number of weapons stolen from a gun shop in Parkersburg. The gun that Fred had was stolen from that gun shop. After many interviews with people, the only logical suspect for the gun seemed to be Earl. They thought about Jimmy Critchlow for a while, since he was Fred's best friend. You were also a suspect." She laughed.

"What's so funny?"

"When the gossipers got to the police they said you were hanging around my house at odd hours. I convinced Charlie that you were sympathizing with me and comforting me. He accepted that, especially when I told him who I hung out with was not really any of his business. Now that things have changed, who I hang out with is now his business.

March 17 Saturday, St. Patrick's Day

It was eight o'clock when Flint walked into the club building carrying a large plastic sack with the bear costume in it. The trio of accomplices were waiting there, Earl Hazzard, Floyd Maynard, and Jimmy Critchlow. Flint looked into Jimmy's eyes quickly and glanced away to face Earl.

"Mavis was taken to the emergency room at the Clarksburg hospital about two hours ago. She called me and I went down to see the situation. She was vomiting and had stomach and chest pains. She told me where to get the bear costume and I have it here. She said she would be willing to take another assignment in order to justify the money and she hoped someone else would take this assignment for today."

Earl thought awhile and asked Flint if he thought Mavis was really sick. Flint assured him she was white as a sheet, her eyes were sunken and had black rings around them.

Earl said he didn't want to cancel the hit. He pulled a fancy cell phone out of the jacket he was wearing and punched a few numbers. He said he was calling the hospital. If Mavis was feeling up to it they could get her and take her to the parade and she could still do her job. Was he really checking to see if Flint was telling the truth.

Earl held the phone up to his ear and waited for an response.

179

"I"m calling about a person who was taken to the emergency room this morning, a few hours ago. My daughter. Her name is Mavis Harper. Would it be possible to talk to her?" pause "I see." pause "Yeah, I will call back this evening."

Earl turned to the three men, "She is in the emergency ward and they are running tests on her. Damn it, damn it."

Flint asked in a serious voice. "Where's the vest. Maybe one of us could wear it and do the job." Floyd Maynard said that was a good idea. He could do it. Earl said it was hanging up in the metal clothes closet in the back room. It was too small for any of them to wear. They might be able to strap it on under their coats and rush up to the speaker's platform and detonate it, but he knew that security there was at a maximum and anyone suspicious wouldn't get within fifty feet of the stand. That's why it was important to have Mavis in the costume.'

"We all are too big for the costume, I agree." Flint was about to play his hand. He addressed Earl "You and Mavis are the same height. You could fit into the costume. I could drive you to Oglebee Square before the speakers got started. You could go over to the university band, don't say anything and then do some crazy shaking, then rush up to the speaker stand and blow them to smithereens."

"And myself with them."

Floyd Maynard didn't know he was playing into Flint's hands. "Yeah, Earl, then you would be famous, like Timothy McVcigh and David Koresh."

Jimmy Critchlow chimed in. "We will build a twenty foot monument to you on these grounds and every meeting have a worship ceremony in your honor. "

180

Flint took the costume out of the bag and held it up to Earl who was now standing. "Yeah Earl, you will fit into this easily. The height is critical, but the sides are floppy and can hold you and the vest. I think you should do it."

"I have a wife and two boys to think of. Let's put it off and wait for another opportunity."

"Mavis was going to do it and she has a daughter. If we really believe in this, you should do it." said Flint in all seriousness.

Floyd Maynard was spastic. "We believe in you Earl. You said this was the most important thing we could ever do as an organization and it was worth sacrificing your life for. Why are you hesitating." Floyd was near tears.

"I am hesitating because I don't want to die."

"Oh Earl," wailed Floyd, "there are some causes worth dying for and this is one of them."

Earl was adamant. "No, I think we should put it off,"

Floyd was almost sobbing. "You let me down Earl, I believed in you. I was willing to kill myself for your cause. You let me down. How could you use me? How could you use Fred Kramer like that?"

"What do you mean by use Fred Kramer like that?" asked Jimmy Critchlow.

Floyd pointed at Earl. "He gave Fred the gun and directions. He told Fred to ask Flint to give him a ride to Charleston."

"Shut up Floyd, that's a command." Earl was in a fighting mood. He had his now famous squirrel expression in his eyes.

Flint still had the costume. "Are you going to get into this

181

costume and let us take you to the parade?"

"No, like I said, I think we should wait for another opportunity."

"That way," said Jimmy, "you won't have to sacrifice yourself and you can get Floyd or somebody else to do it, just like you did Fred Kramer."

"Not me, not anymore," wailed Floyd as he raced out of the room and building. About a minute later they heard a motor starting and a car driving away.

Flint looked at Earl. "I guess there is nothing more to say. I'll take the vest for safe keeping. We can use it at another time. Jimmy and I will call a special meeting of the militia and we will elect a new president, not a commander, a president. And, I expect you to keep out of our way."

"I don't like your stabbing me in the back Flint. Especially after I did you that big favor."

Flint asked, "What big favor. I don't recall any favor you did me."

"Sometimes people don't realize it, when somebody does them a favor."

Earl waved his right arm in the air and brought it down. He didn't say anything more but walked out to his car and drove away as Flint and Jimmy stood looking at each other. When the sound of the motor was no longer heard they shook hands.

Flint smiled, "I have a shovel in the back of my truck."

Jimmy smiled back. "So do I. Where would be a good spot?"

That evening Earl watched the parade and saw the dignitaries on Parkersburg TV. It was the six o'clock news and when it was over he got in his car and headed to the Clarksburg hospital. He asked if it was possible to see patient Mavis Kramer and was informed she was in an intensive care unit of the hospital and she could possibly see him if the nurses on duty agreed to it.

When Mavis was informed that a man was on his way to see her, she assumed it was Earl. She dipped her finger into the black coffee Charlie was drinking and rubbed the liquid under her eyes. It did give them a hollow look.

When Earl arrived on the third floor he had to pass a metal detector which blinked. He was asked to put his car keys and any other metal objects in a tray and he could claim them later. He was led to the room where Mavis was in bed. Officer Charles Fitch was sitting in the chair beside Mavis. He was not in uniform.

Earl said hello to both of them and asked Charlie if he could speak to Mavis alone for a couple of minutes. Charlie agreed and left the room.

"How are you feeling Mavis?" asked Earl with a solemn expression.

"I think okay. They think it's my gall bladder and they might be taking it out tomorrow. I can't stop vomiting."

"You really let us down Mavis."

"I know, and I'll make it up to you Earl. Fred said you would be someone I could rely on and I will do a job for you, after all you paid me in advance."

"That's true. Would it be possible to cancel any future job and get the money back. You can keep the ten thousand I gave you out of my own funds."

"Naw, I don't think so Earl. I already put the money into a trust fund for my daughter. But I will see if I can get it out. It will probably take a while. I would like to do a job, because it's nice to have money. At least for a while."

\

The nurse entered the room. "We will be taking you down for an MRI in about ten minutes. They want to check your head, since your symptoms are compatible with brain problems." Charlie came into the room and looked at Earl. "I guess it's time to leave. Would you like to join me for a cup of coffee in the snack bar?"

"No, I would not." He turned to Mavis. "See what you can do, okay?" He quickly moved through the door.

"What's that all about?" asked Charlie with as much innocence on his face that he could muster.

Mavis had an air of disgust in her voice. "He was responsible for my brother's death and he gave me a lot of money. Now he wants it back. I'm not giving it back, but I didn't tell him that."

The nurse came into the room and started getting the bed ready to move for the MRI. She told Charlie he could wait downstairs if he liked.

"I'm not going to have an MRI, " said Mavis with disgust in her voice. "Get the doctor in here. There's nothing wrong with me but an upset stomach and I want to go home now."

The nurse looked at her with wide eyes. "If it's money you're worried about, your Medicaid card will take care of it."

"No, it's not money. I'm no longer on Medicaid. I feel fine and I want to go home. If you don't get a doctor in here to clear me, I'll be walking out without clearance." She went to the little closet in the room, took off her gown and was only in panties. She began putting on the clothes from the closet. There was no need for modesty with Charlie. The nurse left the room.

"Stick with me Charlie, don't leave me out of your sight. I don't trust this medical staff. We are going to pick up Chloe and go home Charlie." She paused, "to our home Charlie."

25
March 20, Tuesday - Reorganization

The Mountaineer Militia met Tuesday evening. Twenty one of the twenty three dues paying members were there because Flint or Jimmy personally contacted them.

Before the meeting began Floyd Maynard went over to where Flint and Jimmy were huddled and asked, "Is the vest still in the locker?"

Jimmy laughed, "It's sleepin wid da fishes."

Flint was more accommodating. "More like sleeping with the groundhogs. We buried it halfway up the knob in a secluded area away from the firing range. We didn't put it very deep in order to let the weather act on the explosives. It should decay in time. There seemed to be a lot of pellets in it, but that shouldn't interfere with the decay of the paper wrappings and chemicals."

"I was worried about that, I thought Earl might try to still do something with it." Floyd seemed to have recovered from his initial disappointment with Earl. "That guy had me wrapped around his little finger. Boy, was I dumb. I'll never forgive him for what he did to Fred. I'll never forgive him for what he did to me." He repeated. "Boy, was I dumb."

Since Flint was technically the vice president or captain he opened the meeting. "As you have been told, Earl Hazzard has resigned as commander due to personal reasons. So let's nominate people for the position and have a vote. I'll accept nominations at this time. We should have at least two nominees."

Jimmy rose. "I nominate Flint Haloway." Others nodded their approval. Flint said he would have to decline the nomination for personal reasons. He had a lot of his life to sort out and he wouldn't be able to do justice to the club.

Floyd Maynard rose. "I nominate Elmer Atkins." Dan said he seconded the nomination.

Eddie rose. "I nominate Jimmy Critchlow." Coach seconded the nomination.

Ward Hollister moved that the nominations be closed. There was a show of hands and it was approved.

Flint had cut up small scraps of paper and now passed them around. He asked if anyone needed a pencil. Put down EA for Elmer and JC for Jimmy. When the ballots would be counted most of the them would simply have written Elmer or Jimmy on them.

Pencils and pens were shared. Alfie was appointed to collect the ballots. He and Coach would count them. They retired to a corner table. Alfie came back and announced that Elmer had ten votes and Jimmy had eleven, so Jimmy Critchlow would be the new commander and Elmer would be second in charge.

Jimmy moved quickly and suggested they change their name to something less controversial and if that was approved they would change their bank account to the new name. The vote on a name change was 18 to 3.

Dan suggested Mountain State Rod and Gun Club. Eddie suggested Mountain State Outdoor Club. Floyd wanted Mountaineer Gun Club since they were primarily hunters and the fishing was not all that good.

Elmer had an opinion. Why not let everyone think it over and this name change could be decided at the next meeting. He also suggested they get more women involved. "If the name change was acceptable and our goals were more encompassing and perhaps parties were held, we could make this a family oriented organization."

Floyd was serious when he said the club had been a good way to get away from women and their interference with men things. He didn't like the idea of women hanging around.

"It's obvious, we have a lot of different opinions on this subject," said Jimmy. "Why don't we think about this for a couple of weeks until our next monthly meeting. Bring your ideas to that meeting. Think of a name change and whether we want to make this a family oriented organization. We can still have our camp-outs in winter and maintain our shooting range out back. We can still do the spring thaw raft trip. We can discuss political issues if we so desire and we can take a more active role in helping our communities. If we want this to be a family oriented organization we could build an extension on the building and get the kitchen back in shape, maybe add another couple of toilets and wash basins."

Everyone seemed in good humor. They stood around talking. Most of them were pleased with the new direction the organization seemed to be taking. Jimmy was congratulated by Floyd Maynard who said, "Maybe forgetting the past and starting over again is a good idea." Jimmy shook his hand and embraced him. "I'm with you on that buddy."

Meanwhile, behind the club house and up on the knoll along side the rifle range, a vengeful Earl Hazzard eyed the building with loathing. He had a cell phone in his hand. He did not tell his co-conspirators that he had the ability to detonate the vest if Mavis decided she didn't want to do it. He assumed the vest to still be hanging in the metal closet. He punched in the numbers 19323, pressed the pound key, and waited for the explosion. There was none. Did the "company" send him a dud? Maybe he was too far from the building?

Earl moved down the slope a little more, he didn't want to be too close to the building when it was blown to smithereens. He didn't notice the small mound of freshly dug dirt to his left. He punched in the numbers 19323 again and pressed the pound key. The explosion that followed sent Earl into the air and shook the building. The windows were all shattered.

The blast moved mostly upward and the trees around the blast site were now without limbs. Some of the tree trunks attempted to burn. There were no flames on them only a little smoke. Earl was killed outright.

Everyone in the building rushed outside. The smoke and dust from the spot of the explosion was still in the air. Flint yelled, "Everyone stay put, I'll go up and see what happened." He knew what had happened. He walked slowly through part of the firing range and up the knob.

Flint's first thought was that the heat of the earth, spontaneous combustion, had triggered the explosion. Then he saw the battered body of Earl Hazzard. Earl had not stepped on the spot where the vest was buried or he would have been in pieces. Something else must have set it off. He went back to the waiting men. "It looks like Earl Hazzard committed suicide by blowing himself up."

"Someone better notify the Sheriff in Clarksburg." yelled Alfie.

"I'll do that," said Jimmy. "You guys go ahead and look at what happened, but don't touch anything or move anything."

Most of the men walked cautiously up to the site. Flint and Floyd stayed behind. Floyd was crying. "That son-of-a-bitch was going to blow all of us up. He thought the vest was still in the locker."

Flint put his arm around Floyd who turned and put his face into Flint's shoulder. "Only the three of us know that Floyd. Let's let everyone think Earl meant to commit suicide. It's better that way."

Sheriff Ronald Gorman and Deputy Harry Lynch were on the scene in less than an hour. The deputy began unrolling yellow ribbon assisted by Alfie and Dan. They mentioned to the deputy how Earl was always messing with booby traps and land mines and this time he got careless. Deputy Lynch responded. "At around eight o'clock at night and with the rest of you in the building. I don't think Earl would be setting up land mines at this time."

Alfie and Dan agreed with him, but insisted that Earl was going to be ousted as president of the club and it was a position very dear to him and he was probably despondent. The deputy said he would discuss that aspect with the sheriff.

When the situation was stabilized and there was nothing to do but wait for the coroner and the state police forensic team the sheriff asked Flint if he would join him in his car. He said he had asked Flint to join him because he knew that Flint was a leader of sorts in the community. Deputy Lynch would be interviewing some of the others.

"What do you think happened Flint?"

Flint conveyed to the sheriff that he hadn't had much time to think about it, but he thought that Earl had committed suicide by blowing himself up. He was being kicked out as president of the organization and didn't attend tonight's meeting. Almost all the membership was at the meeting.

"He must not have intended to blow himself up or he would have been on top of the blast. He was obviously off to one side of it."

"Then it must have been an accident. He must have set the land mine and was walking away when it detonated. He was always messing with land mines and booby traps."

"Why would he be doing that at this hour of the night. Looks to me like he had set the land mine up during the day and came back at night for some reason and couldn't find where he had placed it. How would it go off?"

Flint was happy for that explanation.

"I don't know, can only guess. How about this? He was upset because he was losing his power over the militia and he wanted a demonstration. He set up the explosion as a protest and was going to set it off with a detonating device after he got out of range of it. Maybe you'll find a cell phone or something like that. There were twenty one of us members in the building when the explosion occurred."

The sheriff paused. "It's all too sudden. Think about it for a couple of days and then we can go over it and try to make some sense out of it. Deputy Harry will get statements from some of the others testifying that you were all in the building at the time."

26
March 22, Thursday The Final Act

Flint called Sheriff Ronald Gorman around ten in the morning and asked if the sheriff could divulge any information about the explosion and Earl Hazzard. The community members were starting unfounded rumors and he wanted something concrete to tell them.

Sheriff Gorman said he could tell Flint the coroner's preliminary findings. "The materials that were available from the blast seemed unconventional. There was a lot of dirt scattered, some of it on and in Earl so he figured Earl must have put some dirt on it then started walking away when the blast was triggered. If you consider 360 degrees as north and 180 degrees as south the blast hit Earl from an angle of 300 degrees. We did find a cell phone loose so it was not in Earl's pocket or the case on his belt. We confirmed it as belonging to Earl. There was no shovel in the vicinity, so if Earl buried it, why would he bury it, he could have buried it the day before, so the dirt might be just part of the blast which went up in a cone fashion and out a little. Coroner figured in the fact the explosives were slightly underground, if Earl had been ten feet further away he would have been knocked down and injured, but not killed. He said he will probably rule the death accidental, since all of you were in the building."

"That would probably be good," offered Flint, "that way Mary and the kids could collect on the insurance. Earl probably buried it at an earlier time, like we said before, and went back and couldn't find the exact spot." He wanted Earl and an early burial of the explosives set in the sheriff's mind.

"I never considered the insurance aspect of it." mused the sheriff. "Yes, that would be good if the death was ruled accidental and his widow could collect the insurance."

The sheriff said there were a lot of puzzling aspects to the explosion. Among them were cloth materials and the type of explosive material. The numbers on Earl's phone were consistent with the phone being used as a detonator.

"While you're on the phone, any progress on the murder of Marjorie?"

"We are close to coming to a conclusion on that matter. I'll fill you in sometime soon, but not over the phone. All the details haven't been worked out. I think the FBI has all the evidence to link the murder to a specific individual"

"When will they make an arrest?"

"Like, I said Flint, I don't like discussing this over the phone."

The length of daylight was getting longer. The winter snow had all melted and the warmth of springtime seemed to be on the way.

Chloe was on the floor in the living room watching television. Mavis and Charlie were getting the supper dishes into the dishwasher. Flint knocked on the door. His face was evident in the small window of the door. Charlie moved quickly to let him in.

"I just wanted to check on a few things with you guys. How is it going?"

Charlie looked pleased. "Couldn't be better,"

Flint wanted to know if Charlie had any new information on the death of Earl. Charlie did not seem surprised by that question. Apparently Mavis had told him of the events and he was playing the cards close to his chest and would deny any knowledge of the events if questioned.

Mavis went to Flint and gave him a hug. "How about some coffee Flint, or maybe a beer. I won't offer you wine because you become wild after a little wine." The attempt at humor was lost due to the seriousness of Flint's expression.

"I will take the beer if you don't mind."

The can of beer and a clear glass mug were quickly put on the table in front of Flint. Charlie poured himself some coffee and sat down at the table.

Flint poured beer into the mug. It fizzled awhile and when it slowed he took the first gulp and swallowed. "Any news on Earl Hazzard?"

"None that we know of." Charlie held his coffee cup in sort of a salute. "No news is good news."

Eventually the conversation got around to the death of Marjorie. That had occurred slightly more than a month ago and yet it seemed like at least a year. When the coroner released the body Flint had it shipped to a cemetery near Pittsburgh for burial in her family plot. It was not a sacred event shared by anyone. There was no family, but she did have two cousins who were notified of her death and obituaries were posted in two newspapers, one in Pittsburgh and the other in Parkersburg.

Charlie said that the investigation of the murder was moving slowly but surely. Mavis added, "They have high hopes since they found the bullet that killed her in her clothing."

"That was not supposed to be common knowledge Mavis."

She said that Flint was her most cherished friend and she didn't think saying something like that to him would be giving away secrets.

Charlie relented and told Flint that they had the bullet and the shell casing. The shooter had to leave in a hurry and the shell casing was thrown to the front into the snow. There was a large patch of disturbed snow in front of the porch railing and apparently the shooter looked for the casing, but abandoned the idea when he saw the man walking his dog.

This was all news to Flint. The time of the shots. The man walking his dog in the early hours of Sunday morning. Charlie added, "The man with the dog also identified Earl's car driving away about five minutes after the shot."

"We are looking for the owner of a nine millimeter handgun. Do you know of anyone that has such a gun? Since you know most of the people around here who have guns. Sheriff Ronald Gorman should have asked you that question. I found out about the casing and bullet by accident. I guess they think I'm too close to the

193

investigation to trust me completely."

Flint said he only knew of one person with a nine millimeter. He went on to describe the camp out and the shooting spree. There were three people with handguns firing shots, a 22, a 32 and the nine millimeter owned by Earl.

Charlie wanted to know if Flint could take him to the firing area and maybe they could find some of the nine millimeter casings and compare it to the casing found in Flint's yard. It could be done.

They were interrupted by Chloe who came over to the table and looked up. "Fint."

"Yes, it's Fint," laughed Flint as he picked Chloe up and held her on his lap and kissed her on the head. "Oh, how I love you little one."

Charlie went back to the topic. "When could you take me to the site so we can search for the casing. Since Earl had the only nine millimeter there, and we got a match, that could be significant."

This was indeed a matter of significance. Flint would take off work on Friday, which was tomorrow and make up the work on Saturday.

Before he left the house, Flint removed a card from his pocket. It had the label on it from the package given to Mavis by Flint who had gotten the package from Earl. "There is no way that Mavis can be involved with this because it was shipped to Earl, as you can see. Maybe you can trace it back to its origin and discover who finances these operations. You don't want to divulge where you got it because you don't want your sources to dry up."

Charlie took the card and said he would consider it if he was certain Mavis would be in the clear. He had surreptitiously checked the legal aspects of the Mavis largesse and found there was no way she would lose it.

March 23 Friday

Sheriff Ronald Gorman, Officer Charlie Fitch and Deputy Harry Lynch picked Flint Halloway up at his house in the police station wagon. Flint remarked that the neighbors would get a lot of mileage out of that. He should have driven to the Clarksburg barracks. "Oh hell, give them something to brighten up their dull lives." Charlie assured him their lives were not dull.

It took forty five minutes to get to the bottom of Camp Mistake Hill. When the deputy was going to drive up the abandoned logging road Flint warned him against it. They all got out and started up the hill that was often referred to as a mountain. "It's only about a half mile to the site." encouraged Flint to Sheriff Gorman who was already gasping for breath.

On the way up the hill the sheriff asked Flint if he had any ideas on the shooting of Marjorie. He said the FBI was in on the case and they thought they had it figured out.

Flint related the story that Earl said he had done Flint a favor and when Flint asked him what favor he replied "sometimes a person will do you a favor and you don't realize it."

Once at the top of the hill and in the open they could see the decayed building of Camp Mistake. Flint halted the march and pointed out the high points of the site, where they had slept out around the campfire which was now a mass of wet black ashes and half burned wood. He told them how he had slept in the building and when he came out in the morning everyone in their sleeping bags were covered with snow. Deputy Lynch said that sounded like fun and would it be possible for him to join their organization, not as a cop, but as an outdoors man.

He would be welcome. The organization would no longer be politically oriented but would be more of an outdoor club. There was

195

some talk about inviting women to participate. They had a new president now and he had big plans for expanding their social activities.

They gathered around the remains of the camp fire. Flint pointed to the house. "We set up beer cans at the base of the sandstone foundation. The rifle shooters stood about a hundred and fifty feet away." He moved his hand back toward the spot. "The pistol shooters were about fifty feet, over there."

He led the group to the approximate area of the pistol shooters. They milled around and finally Officer Fitch said, "Here's some casings over here. Looks like all 22s."

A diligent search found more casings, some of them 32s and nine millimeters. No one picked them up. Deputy Lynch said the weather had probably removed any fingerprints. If it came to court, was Flint willing to testify to these facts about who had which guns and where they were fired. Flint said he would and they could count on Jimmy Crtichlow for back up, even though Jimmy was not present when the casings were picked up. Other members of the militia who were present would also be able to testify if needed.

Small paper bags were produced and the shell casings that were found were put into the different bags according to caliber.

They were on their way back to the Buckeye Patch. Deputy Lynch again told Flint to keep him in mind when the mountaineer club was meeting again. Flint told him about two rafts they were building that would take them down the Kanawha River sometime in April.

"Did you ever call that waitress, what was her name?" Flint said, "Louise, no I haven't, but I will eventually. Don't try to cut me out. I could certainly use some feminine company these days."

Lynch said that after he and Flint talked to Louise he kept wishing it was he who made to offer to call her. He kept thinking about her musical voice and the way those eyes sparkled. Flint again told Lynch not to try to cut in. Lynch said he thought everything was fair in love and war.

They stopped for the usual coffee and doughnut, the lifeblood of police. Sheriff Gorman said he would confide something to Flint since he seemed to be a confidant of Charlie. The FBI had been tailing Earl Hazzard ever since Fred Kramer met his unfortunate death. Earl had a garage storage unit rented on the outskirts of Parkersburg. The FBI entered the unit, with a warrant of course, and found a cache of stolen guns from the same robbery of the gun that Fred had in his possession. They also video taped Earl going into the unit and leaving. He rented the unit under an assumed name, but the clerk in charge identified him by his photograph. If we didn't get him for murder of Marjorie, we will at least have got him on the stolen gun charge.

"Why didn't they arrest him as soon as they found the cache?"

"The FBI wanted to film him entering the storage unit using his key, frisk him and then arrest him. They had all the communication in place to do this. All they needed was for Earl to show up. We expect the pistol that shot Marjorie is there."

"What happens now?"

Sheriff Ronald Gorman indicated he wanted another cup of coffee and another doughnut. "We, along with the FBI, will present our evidence to the coroner and I am certain he will declare Earl Hazzard the murderer of Marjorie and the case would be closed. Why would Earl want to murder Marjorie?"

Flint finished his doughnut. "I missed a lot of militia meeting and this probably made Earl mad. He was a little looney, you know. He probably thought I wanted Marjorie out of the way and that would get me more involved with his militia plans. She was also involved with another militia member and Earl liked to have control

197

over his troops."

"Sounds, crazy, but plausible." agreed Charlie.

When they left Flint off at his house, Charlie said he would get out also and go home for awhile. He never said out loud that he was no longer worried about Mavis and Chloe being alone in the house now that Earl was no longer on the loose.

After the van had pulled out, Flint said Charlie could go to work and he would go over and stay with Mavis until Charlie got back in the evening.

Charlie said that wasn't necessary, he would stay with Mavis for the rest of the day and the weekend. He said, "You know Flint, you were probably in more danger from Earl than Mavis."

March 25 Sunday

Flint had stayed up late into the night watching television. He had worked extra hours on Saturday to make up for the missing Friday. Saturdays in Grafton with Michelle seemed out of the question at this time, maybe for all time. He had promised to take Mildred and Chloe over to see the sheep ranch around two in the afternoon.

At two o'clock he picked up Mildred and Chloe in his pick up truck and drove the two miles to the Hollister Ranch. There was a lot of wonderment in the eyes of little Chloe as she touched the sheep.

Miriam greeted them with refreshments. Ward was in the barn moving things around and getting rid of soiled hay.

When Millie walked out of earshot with Chloe, Miriam asked, "Getting any Flint."

"Naw, that great session with you was all I've done for the last six weeks. I would certainly love to have a repeat on that."

"It was great Flint, but a repeat is out of the question. What's with the lady in Grafton?"

"There's another guy in the picture, who is more suited to her than me, so I graciously stepped out of the way." He looked deep into her eyes. "Are you certain you don't want some more fantasy Miriam?"

"No, Flint, great as that was, you were at the right place at the right time. Just consider it one of those moments in time that can be cherished. I do cherish it."

Millie and Chloe moved back into earshot and so the conversation was shifted to other topics.

When Flint brought Millie and Chloe back to Mavis, Charlie had news. "The FBI had all their charges in order and were about to arrest Earl. They figured Earl knew about it and that's why he took out an extra insurance policy and blew himself up. The insurance company won't be able to prove it was suicide so Mary and the boys will get the money. They might even get a statement from Mary about Earl's activities on the night of the murder. She confided to Edna that Earl was not at home the night that Marjorie was gunned down. It is a moot point now."

"I really feel sorry for Mary and the boys. All of this was unnecessary, but it seemed like Earl wanted fame. I suppose he'll get it now."

It was dark when Flint left the Kramer and Fitch household. It was also Sunday evening. Since he was dressed in his Sunday finery, work shoes, denim pants and shirt, he was set to go somewhere, but where.

He picked up his cell phone, took a folded slip of paper out of his shirt pocket and punched out a number.

"Hello."

"I would like to speak to Louise if I may."

"This is Louise."

The End As Well As A Beginning

Other similar works by the author from Amazon, or Kindle include: *Murder on Wilbur Ridge – Cult of the Blood – In The Kingdom of Kochin – The Identity Thief- The Search for Emerald Mountain – The Boxer College Murder – The Dead Man's Spouse – Ivan Ivanov, Survival in Stalin's Russia – The Incident at Natasova and the Battle of Poltava – Sun Rise Over Peoria – The Witches of Leone Manor - and more.*